THE DOVE AND THE RAVEN

Book One of the Dove and the Raven Saga

Ian Henderson

HENDYBOOKS MEDIA

CONTENTS

CONTENTS

Chapter One

A BRIDGE TOO FAR

NEW YORK CITY - TWO YEARS AGO

M y best friend tried to kill me the Monday before Christmas.

I won't say I deserved it, but it was sort of my fault.

...Let me back up a tic.

Cari and I had been sharing a two-bedroom flat in New York for almost six years. After that long, I'd seen her at her best and worst in equal measures. Not that I'm any saint, mind, but—well, you'll see.

Cari's favourite pop metal album was audible a foot from our front door as I approached, making me wince. I don't mind her taste in music, but not at that volume.

I tapped my key stub against the reader, prompting a flash of teal light as the door clicked and swung open. The sonic assault of *Heartless* intensified. I winced, pulling the door shut as I stepped through into our little foyer.

Across the living room, Cari was seated on our white suede couch, tapping away at her tablet's keyboard. She was sat cross-legged with the old burgundy pillow perched in her lap, supporting her tablet. My best friend's damp hair, dark as coffee grounds, was piled into a bun atop her head. I caught a whiff of my perfume as I got closer.

There was no sign of her tumbler of scotch on the glass coffee table, though.

She's finally starting to heal. Maybe I'm getting through after all.

Cari glanced up as I approached the couch. One hand flew out, adjusting the apartment's holographic stereo controls floating just above the arm of the couch.

"Sorry to assault you like that," she said over the music. "I didn't know when you'd be back."

"I didn't know myself," I said, hiding my surprise. It had been months since Cari'd been anywhere near this cheery—not since her doctoral graduation ceremony.

My best friend turned her attention back to her tablet, typing away. "Clinicals run short?"

"Virtual client meeting got cancelled," I said, setting my knapsack next to the couch. "One of the Knightsbridge investors is holding a soirée on Friday and I made the guest list. We're postponing until after."

"Right, clinicals are Tuesday and Thursday. I forgot."

"Since when have you cared so much about my schedule?"

I wasn't complaining, exactly. It was more unexpected than anything else. Cari hadn't shown interest in anything outside her beloved mythologies and alcohol since... well, quite a long time.

Cari shrugged. "You and my therapist keep telling me I'm too self-involved. I'm pretending to care a bit more."

I rolled my eyes, brushing away a loose strand of my black hair. "Thanks ever so much. Pity you don't write papers as well as you sass people."

"I never have to write another paper again unless I choose to," Cari said, her hands still flying across her keyboard. She tapped on the screen a few times, then folded the tablet closed and set it beside her on the couch.

Her hazel eyes twinkled as she stared up at me. I nearly took a step back.

Something dark and slimy radiated from her aura, something I'd not felt in a long time. I reacted without a thought, calling up my magic to reach out toward her with invisible senses.

My best friend was bathed in a shimmering field, like an iridescent puddle of oil to my farsight. A sense of pride and raven-black satisfaction radiated out from her, cloying in its intensity.

I let go of my farsight and gasped, feeling my heart speed up.

"Something wrong?" Cari asked, still with the same fake cheeriness.

"There's something wrong with your soul," I managed. "Or your aura, at the least. Have you done something?"

I watched her face as she decided whether or not to lie to me. Her tells were too obvious. I'd seen them most of my life.

Cari leaned forward, as if letting something slide off her shoulders. She patted the e-tablet, still resting next to her on the couch.

"Been doing a lot of thinking and reflecting lately. Your idea of writing it all out was helpful. I'm seeing some things in a whole new light. Even my magic."

The bad feeling in my throat crawled toward my stomach. "Really? The thing you've said for years ruined your life?"

"See, Brooke, that's been part of my problem all this time," Cari said. She rolled to her feet and stretched, which was when I realised she was dressed for going out—long shirt, heavy cargo trousers, and her winter boots.

I put on my porcelain diplomat face and walked with measured steps into the kitchen, opening a cabinet as Cari continued to speak.

"I've been afraid of my own power for way too long. When we first found out about our magic, I couldn't ever get it to work properly because I was freaked out. 'What if someone sees me, what if I hurt somebody?'"

"Those were valid concerns," I said, turning the tap on and letting water pour into the kitchen sink. "I didn't fault your logic. Only our execution of it."

I pulled down a larder-sized jar of pink Himalayan salt, along with several other cooking spices that I set on the countertop. Two good-sized grapefruit sat in a bowl beside the sink.

"I noticed something interesting while reminiscing over my old diary," Cari said. "Every time my powers actually worked like I wanted, I was upset."

This can't be good.

I said nothing, giving her space to explain as her syncopated metal music played on in the background.

"I killed the fat guy in that alley after he beat up David." Her lip twitched when she said his name, but at least it didn't send her into a weepy meltdown. "I incinerated Jack Fraser when he shot Amy, and on the island I—"

"Alright, I get the point," I cut her off. "You think your magic only works when you're angry."

She tilted her head in affirmation. "It just makes sense. I had to suppress everything when I was around my ex. Good, bad, didn't matter. If I didn't react exactly how Chris wanted, I got belittled and abused. So I learned how to keep everything bottled up inside."

This was more than I'd ever gotten out of her before. I regretted it.

"That's not a healthy coping mechanism," I said, willing my hands not to tremble. "You know that, right? I've told you so before."

"You also told me anger needs to be let out sometimes. All those times I let it out, guess what?"

I couldn't hide it any longer. I had to know.

"Cari... what have you done?"

My best friend reached into a pocket and withdrew a small rectangle of navy blue cardstock.

"Your dad gave me this in Bristol that summer. He said if there was ever any way he could make restitution, he would." She wiggled the card between two fingers. "Guess what lowlife was serving a life sentence down at West Lake Penitentiary for rape, domestic battery, and first-degree murder?"

My stomach clenched as a cold feeling spread through my chest. A smirk lifted one corner of Cari's mouth as her irises began to glow with a hellish blue flame.

"Yeah. The guards were eager to let me into the cell to see him, once I Suggested they do so."

"Illusion magic is dangerous, Carissa," I said, temper making my accent crisp and sharp. "Do you have any idea the ramifications of toying with someone's mind that way? It may be part of the reason your dad started showing symptoms of Alzheimer's last winter."

Cari's face returned to normal. As the flame receded, I saw her hazel-green eyes shimmering wetly. She firmed her lips, looking away.

"Yeah. Maybe it is. But I can't risk either of my parents knowing."

"That doesn't make it right," I said. "There are rules for how we're to use our magic, Cari. Rules you can't just ignore to take revenge on someone."

"Says who?" Cari said, her regretful tone replaced with defiance. "I don't recall any magical Ten Commandments or whatever. And anyway, it wasn't revenge. It was closure. Think about it. Amy may have caused one or two problems in our past, but Chris was the real reason my life went to hell."

"And he paid for it, if that list of charges was in reference to him," I replied. The cold feeling travelled lower, settling in my stomach. "He'll spend the rest of his life in prison for what he's done."

"Prison is too good for that selfish bastard!" Cari snapped, her eyes and that weird fiery blue hair of hers flaring to life. "Chris Bryson deserved much more than I gave him. Killing him was a mercy."

I closed my eyes, turning away from her. "And you think that's the right course of action, do you? Surely you know you'll be found out."

"Finding out where Chris was only took half my favour," Cari said. "The other half gets me out of the States in one piece, free and clear."

This is my fault.

She'd taken my advice, all right. Taken it way too damn far. Cari had embraced her pain and anger and run in the opposite direction with it. Vengeance wouldn't heal her heart—only acceptance and letting go would let her move on from the hurt.

I needed to talk her down from this cliff.

"I understand being angry," I said, speaking as though to a patient. "That's valid and I'm glad you've accepted that you feel that way."

"Don't patronise me, Brooke. I'm an adult and can make my own decisions."

"Whatever you're up to, I can't let it continue," I said. "Cari, you need help. This is not the way to deal with your pain."

"What would you know about my pain?"

"I've lived with it almost as long as you have, in fact," I said. "Or did you miss the part where I was right there with you and Amy that summer?"

Muscles in her jaw bunched, the old scar through her eyebrow adding to the menace in my best friend's face. Magic stirred, an invisible tension rippling through the air.

"Shut up!"

I had already begun to move as Cari gathered power and sent a burst of blue fire at me. Her golf ball-sized projectile missed, its heat exploding the jar I'd set on the counter. Pink salt and glass shards went flying—as I'd planned.

"Jera!" I said, channelling my own magic into the bind-rune. A flick of my left wrist sent the coarse pink salt soaring towards Cari, where it clumped together in bands as it wrapped around her body.

Our eyes met. The determination in hers scared me.

"I'm not one of your clinical patients, Brooke," Cari snarled, eyes and hair ablaze as she struggled. "Despite what you think. I don't have to listen to you."

"I wish you would." Hot tears stung my eyes. "All I want is for you to deal with your anger and emotions, not wallow in them."

"Anger is the only reason my magic works," Cari said. "I've finally figured out what my power is for. You can't take that from me."

The air stirred as Cari gathered power again and shattered my binding with a cry of, *"Hagalaz!"*

A chill rippled up my spine. She'd broken the binding casual as breathing, drawing up a great deal more power than I'd thought she had.

I had to stop Cari. If words weren't going to get through to her, perhaps magic was the only way.

I had to save my best friend from herself.

I pictured an angular, S-shaped rune in my mind, then inverted it as I drew up power.

"Sowilo!" I said, thrusting my left hand toward her.

Cari gasped, her knees trembling. I felt the working set in as she stumbled, dropping to the kitchen floor.

"I didn't want to do that, Cari," I said, pain in my chest as I watched her struggling to breathe. "But I need to make you reconsider. This is not the right path."

I hadn't channelled enough power into the inverted healing magic to kill her, just slow her down. That meant I was floored to see Cari push herself to her knees, glaring up at me. The hands she pressed to the floor began to scorch, burning two indelible prints into the fake wood.

"Bad move, Augustine."

I felt the odd sensation of blood draining from my face. She'd never used my real first name before.

"You will forget all about this conversation, and any wrongs I may or may not have done in pursuit of my own freedom."

Magic demands a strong will, if it is to be bent to one's designs. Cari bloody well delivered, and the force of her willpower against mine was suffocating. There was one secret I'd never told her, however.

I knew how to resist the Suggestion.

"I am not your thrall, Carissa Elizabeth Edwards," I said, forcing the words out as I wrapped my mind in magic. "This is another rule broken."

My best friend bared her teeth. "Fine. I was going to be diplomatic, but since you're pushing I'll take the direct approach. *Kenaz!*"

She thrust out her hand, sending a ball of blue fire rippling towards me. Time for another new trick.

"Laguz!"

I swept my left hand in an arc, drawing water out of the sink into a quarter-dome before me. Cari's fireball slammed into my liquid shield with enough force to push me back into the opposite counter. It hurt, but I preferred that pain to a fireball in the face. My shield collapsed into a steaming puddle on the vinyl flooring.

"Did you really just—" was all Cari got out before the grapefruit I'd snatched up hit her in the face with a wet crack. Blood poured between her fingers as Cari screamed.

I lunged forward, pushing off the cabinet behind me into a diving tackle. We fell back onto the living room rug, missing the couch by a hair. I took an elbow to the cheek, snapping my head to one side as we rolled.

"Stop this!" I said. "Please! Don't make me—"

"Kenaz!"

The rune-word came out with a burst of dragon fire from her mouth. I rolled again but it caught the edge of my hair. I kept rolling, smothering the flames. I scrambled to my knees and grabbed Cari's tablet from the couch, chucking it. She yelped as the gadget bounced off her shoulder.

Cari dove at me, smashing me backward through the glass coffee table. Air left my lungs in a huff as I hit the rug, glass bits digging into my back.

"Leave me alone!" Cari snarled. She grabbed the burgundy pillow from the couch and brought it down over my face.

My hands acted on their own, scrabbling through the glass bits for anything to help. The right one closed around a metal rod—one of the table's legs. I gripped it and swung, blind and choking.

Cari screamed as the suffocating pillow came free. I gasped, scrambling to my feet. Cari had collapsed back on the couch seat, now bleeding from both her nose and left temple.

I grabbed my phone from my pocket, swiped across the screen, and sent a single text.

"Hurry."

Cari's half-lidded eyes opened, focusing on me. She flicked her wrist, slurring out the rune word with another fireball. I dropped the phone and lashed out with a booted foot, catching her in the stomach. Cari gave a gurgling cough. Her hands wrapped around my ankle, pulling me off balance. I stumbled, kicking at her with my other foot.

"Stop it!" she snapped. "I don't want to burn this place down, but I will."

I replied with another kick to the ribs, at which she let go. My back and upper arms stung from tiny glass cuts, but I had to keep going. He'd arrive soon. I gripped the metal leg of the coffee table more tightly.

"This is wrong, Cari!" I said, turning to face my battered and bloodied friend. Her eyes still blazed with defiance, literally. In fact, the couch had begun to smoulder where strands of her fiery blue hair had brushed against it.

"Says who?" she snapped. "You and the silver spoon you were born with?"

"You can't just go and murder someone, you stupid git—let alone with magic!"

"It was a fair trade," Cari said, her voice rising. She held up a hand wreathed in blue flame. "His life for my freedom. How many times do I have to say it?"

The front door slid open. Hasebe, wielding a wakizashi in one hand and a compact pistol in his other, cybernetic hand, dashed into the room.

A frozen eternity passed as the three of us stared at each other.

Hasebe was the first to move. He dropped the short sword, steadied the semi-automatic pistol in both hands, and fired. At Cari, obviously.

His first two shots went wide, but the third tore a hole in her shoulder.

Cari screamed, stumbling backward into the glass balcony doors. One cracked from top to bottom. Both were spattered with her blood. Steaming tears spilled from my friend's eyes as she slid to the floor, her body shaking.

"Really? You called in your guard dog?"

"It isn't my fault you're refusing to listen to me, Cari," I said, my voice and heart breaking at the sheer hurt in her voice. The metal table leg clanked as it dropped from my fingers. "I know you've been dealt a hard hand in life, but please. I can help you. Let me help you."

"Don't move!" Hasebe barked, sighting down his pistol.

"Wait, Hasebe," I said, holding up a hand to him. "Give me a moment."

I turned back to Cari, who was now clutching her leg.

"I never wanted this for you," I said, using my gentle, clinician voice again. "Even when we were young, it hurt me to see how much you'd been through already. I'm your best friend, Carissa. The choice you've made is wrong, but not irreparable. Let me be there for you, like I have been for so long."

Cari sniffed, wiping her eyes. Her hand was shaking.

"No."

"What?" My chest tightened.

"You heard me. No one is going to hold me back anymore, Brooke. Not even you. If you ever cared in the first place."

Cari plunged her other hand into the pocket on her leg, coming out with an olive green cylinder the size of her fist. Before I could react, she pressed two buttons on its top and bottom.

The room was engulfed in light and a high-pitched ringing.

Aeons later someone mumbled at me, a babbling stream to my poor ears.

"What?" I murmured back.

"...should have let me shoot her," Hasebe's heavily-accented voice said as my ears came back online.

I forced my eyes open to find my bodyguard standing in front of me, a fire extinguisher clutched in his cybernetic hand.

As my senses recovered, I discovered the couch I'd fallen on was still smouldering, as was the cuff of my right sleeve. I gave an inelegant squeak and jumped to my feet. Hasebe caught me as I stumbled into him and sprayed me with the extinguisher before turning his attention to the couch.

"Sowilo," I said under my breath, focusing my will. The shaking of my limbs told me I'd burned through a fair chunk of my magical reserves, though there was enough remaining to heal my bruises and cuts. My hair was a loss, though. I'd have to run to the salon before Friday's event.

I shook my head, disgusted with myself. How could I be thinking about hairstyles and dinner parties at a time like this?

"Is she still here?" I said, glass crunching under my feet as I moved.

My bodyguard's metal fingers clenched the fire extinguisher's nozzle. "She detonated a flashbang and ran past me. If we move quickly, we can catch her before she reaches the—"

"We both know how quickly that elevator moves, Hasebe," I said, sinking onto the non-burnt part of the couch.

Our little flat was a mess. In addition to the couch, the living room was now decorated with pink salt, broken glass, and splatters of blood. Cari's burgundy pillow that had almost ended my life had been slashed open in the scuffle and lay against one wall. The stereo was still on, just loud enough to be audible.

"Veridia, shut the music off," I said, leaning my head over the couch.

"Okay, shutting off 'Writing Music,'" the smart hub said from the kitchen counter. The music stopped seconds later.

"Six years ago, you gave me a second chance," Hasebe said, breaking the brief silence. "My debt to you is severe. That is not so for your friend. I could break her without a second thought."

"Violence won't solve anything," I said, putting some iron in my tone. "It may work on the schoolyard, but not here. Not with her."

Her magic is too strong for simple violence.

Hasebe set his jaw. I knew if I gave the word he'd rush after Cari in an instant. It may have been the right choice, given her crime. And whatever else she may have done on the way.

I couldn't give the order. I felt too guilty, for one.

How had I missed all the signs? Cari had been heading to the edge of this disaster for months, and I'd cheerily given her the tools to get there. I'd been so focused on her as a project, it had never occurred to me she might choose to find a different message from her past traumas than the one I'd intended her to see.

Cari was more than a project—she'd been the other pea in my proverbial pod for so long she felt like the sister I'd never had. There must have been a better way to reach her. I ought to have known what it was.

If you two were truly as close as you thought, you wouldn't have let her get this desperate.

The accusing voice of my conscience made a good point. I'd grown up with Cari, yes, but when had we grown so distant?

"I'm going to get the stain remover," I said, hoping Hasebe couldn't hear the catch in my voice. "Call the front office, if you would. Let them know we had a small fire in the kitchen and it's nothing to worry about."

Without waiting for his reply, I stood and marched down the hallway to our bathroom, locking the door behind me. My reflection stared back at me, her grey eyes hollow and her pale face spattered with blood. Patches of my black hair were burnt and singed, and the swirling tattoos on my left arm peeked out beneath the burned-off sleeve. I looked worse than I'd thought, but it paled in comparison to the aching emptiness in my heart.

What have I done?

Decorum be damned. I curled up into a ball and sobbed, knees pulled to my chest.

I'd failed. Despite my best efforts, I'd let Cari down. She'd taken action on her own as a result, leading to this disaster of an intervention.

Bone-deep weariness settled over me. It was all I could do to drag myself to my feet minutes later and grab the industrial size bottle of stain remover from the shelves above our laundry machines.

Hasebe was running the vacuum across the living room rug, hoovering up the last of the glass bits. He glanced up as I walked past, dark eyes taking in everything.

"What will you do now?" he said, shutting off the machine.

I brushed tears from my cheeks.

"I caused all this," I said, gesturing to the decimated apartment around us. "It's my fault she went off like that. I forced her hand."

"Perhaps, perhaps not," Hasebe said. "Either way, she is gone."

"Not for long," I said, iron creeping into my voice. "Wherever she's gone, whatever she's done, I'm going to find her. I've got to make this right."

CHAPTER TWO

ON HER TRAIL

JOHANNESBURG, SOUTH AFRICA - PRESENT DAY

S omeone had done an impressive amount of damage.

One corner of the rental shop's roof across the street had been melted in. The husks of three burnt-out vehicles lay in the middle of the street, one just recognizable as a police car. Disfigured patches of the tarred road marked spots where something extremely flammable had made contact with it.

"This is it," I said to myself. "It has to be."

Hasebe heard me anyway. "How can you be sure?"

I gestured at the tarred road. "These aren't from grenades, or flares. There's no residue of propellant or bits of casing."

In fact, I was bluffing. Just a little. I still wasn't certain this had actually been my best friend's handiwork, no matter how hard I wanted to believe it was. We'd been searching for her for two years without anything resembling a lead until a week ago.

I had not expected my lead to look like this.

My God, Cari... what on earth made you do this?

I shook myself and nodded to Hasebe. "Let's go in. Perhaps the desk clerk will be able to tell us what happened."

He made a low sound in his throat, tilting his head.

The two of us stepped off the sidewalk and passed through the line of holographic yellow chevrons ringing the scene. The semi-real icons flickered as I crossed through them.

Ten years ago it would still have been police tape... technology moves so fast.

A well-tanned man looked up as I pushed the door of the rental car shop open, cigarette hanging from his mouth.

"Shop's closed unless you have cash," he said, his accent flavoured much like my own.

"I noticed," I said, flashing a fake INTERPOL badge. "Would you mind telling me what got one of your customers unhappy enough to try and torch your shop yesterday?"

The man took a sharp breath, almost inhaling his cigarette. He coughed and spluttered, jumping to his feet.

"Listen, lady," he wheezed. "It's not my shop and I don't want more trouble. That crazy American chick already has this place shut down for four weeks."

"American chick?" I parroted, diplomat face firmly in place. "What did she want?"

"What do you think? She wanted a desert Jeep. Demanded I give her one. Loudmouth tourist."

"A tourist would not have been able to do that," Hasebe said, gesturing to the melted wreckage outside.

The man rolled his eyes, but he curled one arm around his torso. With his other hand, he reached up and held the cigarette between two fingers as he took a drag.

"Damn right about that. I must have been more drunk than I thought. Her voice went strange and crystalline, and I swear her eyes were glowing blue."

I fought the urge to gnaw at my lip, even as my heart began racing. *Attempted Suggestion, glowing eyes... it fits. At last, a lead.*

"Did she say why she wanted the vehicle, or where she was going?" I asked, keeping my tone professional.

"Out into Kalahari, where else?" he shook his head. "When I told her I wouldn't just give her a Jeep, she pulled a gun and threatened me. Said she'd shoot me through the eye if I didn't hand over the keys."

Hasebe made a noise that wasn't quite a growl. I shot him a quick glance before replying.

"So you did give her the Jeep, yes?"

"You think I wanted to get shot? Of course I gave her the Jeep. But I know what my boss would do to me if I let one get stolen, so I triggered the silent alarm. Cops were here in less than two minutes."

"Impressive response time," I said, sliding my thumb across the screen of my smartphone. It opened the browser app instead of the notebook I'd selected, but I made do.

"Is your vehicle GPS system still functioning?" Hasebe asked.

The clerk shrugged, his striped polo almost masking the movement as he sat back on his stool behind the counter. "I dunno, probably. I haven't checked."

"I suggest you find out," said Hasebe, leaning toward him. "If you have the data from that vehicle, it is possible we may find the culprit."

The clerk sighed, exhaling another cloud of smoke as he flipped open the laptop seated next to him on the counter. "Fine, sure. Not like—"

He blinked. "Well rack me. It's still functioning."

"What does it say?" I asked.

"Sure enough. This baby's thirty miles or so into the Kalahari. Doesn't look like it's moving, though."

"We can still catch her," I said, my excitement breaking through the façade. I dug in my clutch and pulled out a small roll of currency, setting it down on the counter. "Give me whatever vehicle you have available. And the GPS data, if you would."

The clerk glanced from the cash to me and snatched up a set of keys from somewhere beneath his counter, handing them to me along with a microSD card. "Number sixteen, around the corner. Safe travels and all that."

I nodded, my sundress swishing around my calves as I turned and marched out the door.

"The rental cost was a third of what you paid him," Hasebe said in Japanese. "And we already have a vehicle."

"I know," I replied in kind. "But considering how much business the shop is going to lose, I wanted to help out just a bit."

"It is your money, I suppose. There is plenty to spare."

As we walked past one of the burnt-out vehicles, a thought struck me.

"Give me a moment," I said, walking into the middle of the carnage. "I'm going to test one further thing. Just to be certain."

I opened my clutch, extracting a single piece of white chalk. That done, I sketched a rough circle on the road at my feet. It was harder than expected on the old and bumpy asphalt. Once drawn, I stepped inside my circle and drew up my magic.

There are books in almost every language and culture regarding the practice of magic, none of which had stood up to my experiments over the years. Useful information on magic had been almost impossible to come by, save for one recurring element—magic circles had consistently functioned to focus and clarify my power.

I'd tried circles at Stonehenge, the faerie forts in Ireland, even etching one in the basement of the family manor. All of them had worked. It was the only concrete information I'd found, aside from one Victorian-era manuscript on my desk at home and my own inherent knowledge.

So when I stepped into my freshly-drawn circle, magical senses engaged, I was not expecting to be hit by such a nauseating feeling of *wrong*.

Someone had used magic here, that was certain. The electric sensation of it in the air prickled the back of my neck.

Desperation, anger, and a suffocating sensation of emptiness... oh no. I was afraid of this.

The feeling was just how I remembered Cari when we'd been flatmates in grad school.

I'd learned from the Victorian book that magic was empathic, to a degree. It was impossible to do something with magic that you didn't believe in, on some level. One's emotional state at the time of performing a working could influence how stable it was, hence a need for proper focus and a balanced mind.

Instead, the negative emotions flowed over me, bringing tears to my eyes. One of the hologram projectors behind me shorted out in a puff of smoke. The yellow police chevrons disappeared.

"It's her alright," I managed. "No mistaking it."

Hasebe firmed his lips. "I feared as much. If we are going after her, we need more equipment."

"What do you have in mind?"

I didn't want to know what sort of nasty things he might have brought to use against Cari, but I had to admit—the carnage made me nervous. She'd developed a short temper when we'd roomed together. If this truly was her, her temper had gotten even worse since she'd disappeared.

"We can discuss this at the hotel," Hasebe said, holding out his cybernetic hand. I tossed him the Jeep keys.

Minutes later we were on the streets of Johannesburg, dodging traffic on the route to our hotel. I must admit, I was glad Hasebe drove. Driving a car was something I never quite got the hang of, which at twenty-six years old felt terrible to think about. Wealth has its downsides. Put me on a bike or in an aircar, I'm your girl. Cars, that's another story altogether.

Hasebe made it look easy, weaving back and forth as he avoided both other vehicles and pedestrians.

"Take a left here," I said, checking the GPS on my smartphone. It had been acting up as of late, but today the gadget seemed to be behaving.

Hasebe screeched into a left turn. I held on to my phone but it was a near thing. My clutch wasn't so lucky, falling into the Jeep's passenger side footwell. I'd elected to carry the smaller bag in the belief it would be harder to steal.

"Next time, tell me before we're almost past the turn," he said.

"What's got you in such a mood?" I asked, fishing my little purse from the floor. "You've been quite morose ever since we got here."

He was silent for a few moments, pulling up into the hotel's parking garage. Then Hasebe turned to face me, expression unreadable behind his sunglasses.

"My apologies. This place, it... The last time I was in South Africa was with Yoshida-*sama*. Nearly twenty years ago now."

"Ah."

Daiki Yoshida, the billionaire and late CEO of the largest technology company in the world, had once been Hasebe's employer. He was the hostage we'd failed to save all those years ago. I'd bought out Hasebe's contract afterward due in large part to guilt over said failure—it was one of the few things Father had let me choose to spend my own money on at the time.

"I didn't know," I said. "I'm sorry."

Hasebe shut off the Jeep's engine. It made a series of pinging noises as things beneath the hood cooled down

"It is my duty to follow you," my bodyguard said. "But twenty-nine years of bodyguarding has taught me much. My heart does not bleed as yours does."

He got out and went around the car. I opened my door and stepped out just as he arrived. It was a game we'd played for years.

The suite I'd reserved was in fact the resort's penthouse—complete with private elevator, three bedrooms, and a glorious view of the horizon. Off to the right there was the outline of the famous Carlton Centre skyscraper, silhouetted against the afternoon sun.

See this, Father? I invested, earned all this on my own, and didn't even have to resort to shady deeds. Honest wealth has its perks.

My valet, Westaway, had delivered our luggage to the penthouse while we'd been investigating. It sat stacked in a neat pile just inside the kitchen area.

Hasebe snatched up his suitcase and opened it across the dining table, spreading its contents on a cloth he pulled from the case. Rather than clothing or toiletries, my bodyguard had brought a variety of weaponry with him. His case contained three pistols including his favourite Cobalt revolver, a dozen throwing knives in a bandolier, five smoke bombs, and a small blue and yellow handgun I hadn't seen before.

"Moliére is a new handgun manufacturer," Hasebe said, catching me looking at the gun. "I brought that one for you."

There was a sparkle of mischief in his eye. He hit the magazine release and pulled back the slide all with one hand, extending the magazine out to me. Instead of proper bullets, this gun was loaded with metal ball bearings the size of my pinky nail.

I frowned at him. "I know my way around guns, Hasebe. There's no need for kid gloves."

"The 'kid gloves' aren't for you," he said, sliding the magazine back into the handgun. "This weapon fires galvanised pellets, which impart a paralysing, high-voltage shock on impact instead of penetrating the target."

"So it's a taser handgun," I said, accepting the yellow and blue weapon butt-first. "Feels quite nice. I like the textured grip."

"This way you will not feel guilty about shooting Carissa, if we find her here," Hasebe said. "No other weapons company in the world produces anything close to it."

Now I understood. It was as close to a compromise as I was going to get from my bodyguard, loyal as he was.

"Will this fit in a standard shoulder holster?"

"It should," Hasebe said.

I nodded. "I appreciate the thought. Thank you for trying to make sure I don't kill Cari."

"I shouldn't be," he muttered, turning back to his makeshift weapons table.

I strolled to the balcony, looking out over the city. Light glinted off the towering buildings, accented by the cacophony of the city I heard even from up here. It reminded me of the view from our fifty-third floor flat in New York, back in grad school. Johannesburg's skyline was interrupted here and there by flashes of greenery, which did make a marked difference from the New York place.

My fingers tightened on the railing.

"Cari, what the hell are you doing here?" I said, letting out a long exhale. "Why Africa, of all places?"

"Has it occurred to you," Hasebe said, stepping up beside me, "that your interest in finding Carissa could be unhealthy? Perhaps obsessive?"

"You think I haven't considered that?" I said, turning to face him. Hasebe had grown out a long topknot in the last year, which was starting to show streaks of grey. Sweat had plastered his linen shirt to his broad shoulders, but he didn't seem to notice.

"I think you might be better served going to parties, or visiting Savile Row, or whatever it is rich women your age do these days."

I rolled my eyes. "Don't start, Hasebe. Father's been giving me that line for twenty years now, ever since I was old enough to speak my mind. I don't want to be like my peers. Or him."

He shrugged. "I know. But it would be safer than this fool's errand. Carissa does not want to be helped."

"That doesn't mean I'm not going to try," I said. "We met when we were little girls and she'd just lost someone important to her. Cari was a bright spark who went through some awful things."

I shook my head, leaning against the railing. "I can't excuse what she did, it was wrong, but despite all her flaws she's just a traumatised little girl who needs help."

"A traumatised little girl who has power enough to rival Amaterasu," Hasebe retorted. "You diplomats are all the same. You think words will solve problems only violence can."

"Humor me," I said.

Hasebe's jaw clenched beneath his trimmed beard. "I will accompany you, but it would be remiss of me to not give voice to my concerns."

"And that is not lost on me, make no mistake," I said, looking him in the eye. "You've always been a voice of calm in my life, Hasebe. But this is something I feel responsible to resolve. I created this mess, and I will stop her if necessary."

"Are you prepared for confrontation?"

I closed my eyes, looking inward. My magic sparkled and tingled inside, flickers of electricity in the high tension wire that was my nervous system.

"Charged and ready for whatever comes," I said, opening my eyes.

"I did not mean your *yokai* talents. Are your heart and soul prepared for what may be required?"

I couldn't meet his gaze, looking back out over the city instead.

Chapter Three

THE MAN WITH GOLDEN EYES

After changing into more appropriate adventuring garb, we set off into the desert. The sun was beginning to dip below the horizon, painting the sky in pink and orange hues visible even from amidst the skyscrapers.

I finished braiding my hair and pulled out my laptop, slotting in the microSD card. A sat-nav window appeared on the screen, tiny Jeep silhouette pulsing near the edge of the Kalahari.

"Well well... it's been eight years since I Drowned," I murmured, catching a glimpse of the date stamp in the bottom of the screen. "I nearly forgot."

"Drowned?"

"I waded into a pool on that Celtic island and sucked down a lungful," I said. "Had no idea what I was doing, but the magic did. That was the day I gained my powers, almost a week after the other two."

"Ah. You mentioned that before as though it was a special circumstance."

"It was, I suppose. Drowning marks the rebirth of those who've been awakened to magic, as melodramatic as that sounds."

"I know Carissa kept her power secret. Did you?"

"I almost told Mum," I admitted. "Think it would've come as too much of a shock for her. There was no way I was telling Father. I finally had power and resources that didn't come from him."

Hasebe nodded, adjusting his sunglasses as he drove. "So you will be underestimated by your opponents. A wise tactic. Have you decided what you will do if we find her?"

I shook my head, black braid flopping over one shoulder. "My mind keeps spinning, Hasebe. Too many what-ifs, too many I-shoulds."

"Do not let your mind become clouded. If action becomes necessary, a clouded mind can only lead to failure."

Again, I added to myself.

That was one thing I was sure of—I wasn't going to fail. Not this time.

Despite the setting sun it was quite warm this far into the outdoors, which made me glad for the vehicle's aircon. Hasebe didn't seem to mind the heat—or if he did, he kept to himself.

I kept my laptop open on the centre console, keeping an eye on the tracking data as he drove.

"Africa is not a place I would expect ancient Vikings to be," Hasebe commented. The Jeep's engine revved as we crested a dune.

"Nor I. I seem to recall Cari once saying something about Viking settlements in northern Africa, around the Mediterranean. Nothing remotely close to here."

The steering wheel squeaked as Hasebe's cybernetic hand tightened around it. "Then this could be a trap."

"If Father's enemies wanted to go after me, they'd have plenty of other chances before now," I said. "And Cari... well, that's what we're here to find out."

Hasebe didn't reply, leaving me with time to think. Would Cari really have stooped so low as to get in a fight with the police and threaten a shopkeeper over a car?

She's already murdered someone. There's hardly a less sacred line she could've crossed.

I clenched my teeth until my jaws hurt. Regardless of her missteps, I still believed in my best friend. It was my role to save her from herself, whatever she'd done and wherever she was.

A dark blur shimmered into view ahead, perched atop the dunes. I glanced at my laptop, then gestured to the blur.

"I think that's our missing Jeep."

Hasebe tilted his head, steering our car in that direction. Sure enough, the blur resolved into a dark blue desert Jeep much the same as our own.

The closer we got, the stranger I felt. It was as though I'd rubbed my feet against a thick carpet and walked through a room of balloons. The air was charged with an electric current... one I recognised.

"Be on guard," I told Hasebe. "I've got an odd feeling about this. There's magic at play here."

"She is here?"

"It certainly isn't Amy. Last I knew she was living in the Pacific Northwest."

Hasebe glanced at me, my pale but flushed face reflected in his sunglasses.

"I don't like this. Why would she abandon the vehicle but leave its positioning tracker active?"

"She may not have known it was there," I said. "Everyone can make mistakes."

Hasebe pulled out his Cobalt revolver, thumbing back the hammer as he pulled up beside the missing Jeep. I slid out and began inspecting the vehicle, looking for any signs of my friend. Sand had blown over its seats, suggesting we were at least a day behind. Other than that untidiness, the vehicle was in perfect condition.

So much for the physical. It was time for the metaphysical approach.

I closed my eyes, reaching inside for my magic again. My senses sharpened, acutely hearing my own breath and the wind whistling past my ears. The electric tingle of magic grew stronger, but more concentrated. Instead of a static cloud, this sensation was a looming thunderstorm.

Hasebe let out a startled exclamation in Japanese. "Down there!"

I glanced down to see what he was looking at and nearly fell across the Jeep's bonnet.

There, at the base of the dunes, was a Viking longship.

Most of the ship was still intact, laying half-buried in the sand on one side. A large hole had broken through the middle of the ancient ship's hull, more than big enough for someone to have crawled through.

Despite being weathered the wood was in good condition, though the shields mounted along the visible side of the longship had been bleached of their colours. With my magical senses still engaged, the source of the magic became obvious. Someone was inside the ship.

"Cari!"

I hurried to the edge of the dune and began to slide down, grateful for the tall boots I'd selected.

"Wait!" Hasebe called after me, but I'd come too far to turn back now. I kept my footing and hurried toward the longship. I stumbled the last few steps, throwing out my hands to avoid clocking my head against the ship's stern. My outstretched hand went through the wood as though it wasn't there.

A horrible thought struck in that flash of not-quite contact.

Jera. The bind-rune can also be used to bind energy into something... such as an illusion.

"*Hagalaz!*" I said, sweeping my hand through the fake ship.

It held for a moment before bursting apart into a dazzling cloud of fractal shapes. In its place was a cluster of figures in dark green cloaks.

Another person appeared in front of them. I don't mean it came into view—the figure was not there, then it was.

The man was too broad and tall to be Cari, standing head and shoulders above the others. He wore a tailored grey suit, its cut suggesting a Reiss. His face was more rugged and weatherworn than I would've expected for someone with that kind of money, accented by a thick brown beard and topknot shot through with grey.

More striking than all that, though, were his golden irises. They were exactly like mine when I called on my magic, only his seemed to retain that colour at all times.

"You're contained now, *seidhkona*," he said, speaking English with a heavy dash of Scandinavia. "Try to escape and I will crush you."

"I am no witch, sir," I said, halfway between formal and outraged. Who the bloody hell was this guy, and why was he using Old Norse words to insult me?

"Nice try, Juno. You won't fool me. Keepers, surround her."

The green-cloaked figures began to move, forming a V-shape with the tall man at the point of the V.

Ten, counting the big man. These are not good odds. I wish I'd brought my knives.

"Whoever this Juno person is, I can assure you I'm not her," I said, hoping my diplomat's face held. This massive man was the thunderstorm. He was the immense source of power I'd felt, not Cari. Did that mean there were others out there with magic? If that was true, it changed everything.

"Don't lie, *seidhkona*," the big man said, spitting on the sand. "I can feel your power, though it is nothing compared to my own. The both of us know you're responsible for the dark magic in Johannesburg, and taking the life of a lawman. Among many other crimes I won't name."

I didn't like the direction this was beginning to go. "Surely you sensed the emotion in the magical residue of that place, if your power is so strong. Are those emotions truly how I feel? Is your farsight so clouded?"

"What do you know of farsight?" the big man said. "Is it a word you read in a book somewhere?"

It was, but I didn't feel the need to admit that.

"I know enough to know that witchcraft is evil," I replied. "Enough to know I'd never dare do it for fear of corrupting myself."

"Yet you've fallen right into my trap," the big man said, raising his left hand. "I predicted Juno would come, and here you are."

"One move and you die!"

Hasebe's voice rang out over the scene like two broken bones grating together. I glanced over my shoulder to see him perched atop our Jeep's bonnet, training his Cobalt revolver on the big man from above.

Clint Eastwood would be proud—maybe I'll tell Hasebe that later, if we survive.

The other nine figures—Keepers, he'd called them?—reached beneath their dark green cloaks and drew out honest-to-God flintlock pistols. I couldn't suppress a startled laugh.

"Who the hell are you people, a group of cosplayers?"

"The only playing here is on your part, Juno," the big man replied. "And I tire of it. Keepers—shields up. Morgana wants her taken alive."

"Elkhaz," nine voices choroused. Flat rectangles of teal light shimmered into existence before each of the green-cloaked Keepers as magic crackled through the air.

I thought a very rude word. Our odds had gone from bad to impossible—ten powerful magic users versus myself and Hasebe. I'd never seen someone perform a shield working before. I knew it was possible, but the mechanics were beyond my ability. More mysteries piling on top of each other, if we survived the next several minutes.

Even so, I would not submit without a fight.

"Very well then," I said, calling up my magic. "You've forced my hand. If I am to defend myself, so be it. *Uruz!*"

I thrust my left hand at the ground, fingers splayed, then threw it into the sky. A cloud of sand matched my motion, filling the space with a whirling maelstrom of tiny particles. I was again glad I'd opted for proper trousers instead of the sundress for this second outing.

An engine revved on the dune behind me. I spun to see Hasebe, now behind the wheel of our Jeep, careening down the steep slope. I raced towards the Jeep, squinting against my impromptu sandstorm.

The big man had seen him too. His booming voice rang out above the swirling sand. *"Uruz!"*

My diversion collapsed, forming into thin walls of sand on either side of me. I didn't slow down. Nor did Hasebe. The Jeep raced toward me over the sand. I dove into its backseat, twisting around to look back at our attackers.

Gunshots rang out as the Keepers fired, sending up small clouds of smoke with each shot. Hasebe returned fire, wrenching the wheel with his other hand as he sent the Jeep into a sharp about-face.

"Uruz!" I shouted, thrusting out my left hand in a scooping motion. The sand responded to the force rune in a wave, hurtling straight into the Keepers and sending them to the ground.

The big man sidestepped the wave of sand, twisting his fingers as he barked, *"Isa!"*

A wall of ice exploded out of the sand in front of our Jeep like a hydraulic road barrier. Hasebe slammed the brakes, twisting the wheel so hard he cracked it. The Jeep turned but its back tyre smashed full into the ice on one side, sending me hurtling over the short wall.

Damn it, not again!

I rolled into the fall, coming up on my feet with the ice separating me from Hasebe and the Jeep. One of the Keepers popped out from behind the wall, hand outstretched. Another wall of ice sprang up, followed by a third and a fourth.

I bared my teeth, calling deeply on my magic. Though it mostly broke the laws of physics, there were still practical applications with my power. Uruz was not a rune that only controlled sand or earth—it was a rune of pure force.

"Uruz!" I cried, thrusting my hand toward the sand. Invisible force smashed into the ground below me, its equal and opposite reaction sending me flying over the icy barricade at a steep angle.

More shots ripped past me, going wide. It had been a good dodge, but I'd overcompensated. Fatigue swept through my body as though I'd run two back-to-back marathons.

Hell... not used to expending this much magic all at once...

I tried to hit the sand on my feet but my legs betrayed me, sending me flopping to the ground. I struggled to my feet, fighting my weary limbs as the Keepers hurried toward me.

Drawing the garish taser handgun from my shoulder holster, I flicked the primer switch as I took aim at the nearest Keeper and fired.

The young woman cried out and collapsed twitching to the sand as the electrified pellet hit her shoulder. My next shot went wide, missing the second Keeper by at least a metre.

Something slammed into my back, taking me to the sand. I coughed and spluttered, spitting sand out of my mouth as a pair of dark leather brogues came into view.

"Formidable trickery, Juno," the big man said, kneeling down as he spoke. "But it will not save you. You are under arrest for crimes against the White Order and violation of its nine laws."

"I'm not Juno, you ignorant git!" I snapped, spitting more sand. "Must I keep repeating myself?"

A pair of thick cuffs snapped around my wrists, straining my shoulders as my arms bent backward at an odd angle. I was hauled to my feet and gagged with a handkerchief of the same dark green cloth. It tasted odd, almost minty.

Hasebe had been similarly restrained, though a dark bruise on his cheek told me he'd not gone quietly either.

"You will be brought before the Althing for judgement, as is custom," the big man intoned, his voice grave. I also picked out an odd note of relief in his words. Just who was this Juno that had these people so worried? And why were they working for the Icelandic government, any road?

"Raidho."

The big man swept his left hand in an arc over his head. I gasped as a glittering rainbow followed the arc of his hand before dissolving into a nauseating blur of colours that swept across the sand.

I forced my eyes shut, trying to keep breakfast in its place. The temperature dropped significantly, sending a shiver up my back. Magic engulfed me, so dense and stifling I started to choke through the gag. Rough sand under my cheek turned to cold wood. My nose filled with the scent of the sea, far more calming than the circumstances warranted.

Gloved hands pulled me to my feet. I opened my eyes to find myself standing on an old wooden dock, next to Hasebe and the green-cloaked Keepers. The big man stood a few paces away, looking out over the sea at a bustling city in the distance.

I hadn't seen the city in some time, but it was a silhouette I recognized.

The big man had brought us to Reykjavik.

CHAPTER FOUR

FLICKERS OF SUSPICION

REYKJAVIK, ICELAND

I 'd visited Reykjavik only once, earlier this year.

An old acquaintance from boarding school had been short a guitarist for his gig at the Iceland Airwaves music festival back in January and had reached out after seeing some videos I'd put up online. I hadn't thought my playing all that impressive, but it did the trick. Under the pseudonym 'Lady Fingers,' I'd played five shows in three days with his band, Death in the Family. My punk teenage self would have died from happiness.

It had been an incredible experience, but one that had not left me time to explore the old city much. Yet even during my brief visit, Reykjavik had felt old, an aged grizzly bear deep in hibernation. Despite its hustle and bustle there was something very Old World about the place.

I didn't want to see it again like this.

"Come," the big man said, gesturing over his shoulder as he began walking across the dock toward a wooden pathway. He whispered something under his breath as the Keepers shoved us forward and magic stirred around us again. This time, it was a... well, a fuzzy sort of magic, I suppose. It's hard to put into words, but this working felt as though a heat blur surrounded my body.

I shot a glance at Hasebe. He'd lost his sunglasses somewhere in the scuffle, and the glance he gave me could have defrosted a glacier. I nodded, trying to convey as best I could that he'd been right. It had been a trap, but not for us.

Who is Juno? And why do they think so strongly that it's me?

For a moment, the horrible thought that Juno might actually be my best friend crossed my mind. I dismissed it just as quickly. Cari wanted to be left alone, not pick fights with some secret group of wizards. It was part of why she'd been so damned hard to find.

I reached up to pull the handkerchief out of my mouth and was rewarded with a jab between the shoulder blades for my trouble. I managed to yank the gag away just long enough to gasp in a breath.

"Where are you taking us?"

"The last place you'll ever see," the big man replied from in front of me.

"Aren't you being a bit dramatic?" I said. "Surely there's some sort of—"

"There is not anything left for you, Juno. Only your punishment."

Before I could protest, the big man whispered something again. Power gathered around my face as the handkerchief was shoved back up into place by invisible force.

Hasebe growled, clenching his teeth around his own gag. I didn't blame him.

His metal fingers twitched at his side in a short code phrase—*action?*

Play along, I gestured back, not knowing what else to do. We were out of options, and I was critically short on magic. My limbs were still trembling from overexertion.

Hasebe closed his eyes and nodded slowly.

After a short trip on a fishing boat, we arrived at a small island off the northwestern coast of the city. The island was mostly grassland, a few buildings and other structures dotting the landscape. One stood out—a white wooden building with three windows on one side and a small steeple extending from its roof.

Is that a church? Why would they be taking us there?

A brief hike brought us to the building, which an informational plaque outside the door proclaimed to be Videyjarkirkja Church, or Videy Church for short. The tiny building had been built in the late 18th century, which was all the further information my quick glance provided. The big man had to turn sideways, but he fit through the door into the old church as the Keepers filed in around and behind us.

There was an odd sense of peace in the place, bolstered by the worn, teal-painted wooden pews and the closeness of the room. Under other circumstances, it would have been a right lovely bit of history.

To the right of the altar, a wooden confessional chair stood just beside an alcove set back into the wall. The big man stepped over the barrier ropes and strode to the recessed alcove. He reached into the pocket of his suit coat and extracted a thumb-sized piece of chalk. With a calligrapher's precision, he sketched an angular shape on the alcove's wooden frame, then drew a circle around it. I was too far away to make anything out, even if I'd been able to focus properly. That skirmish in the desert had drained me to a worrying degree.

Power stirred in the air around the chalk sketch, a shower of rain instead of a thunderstorm. Nothing obvious happened, save for a flicker of light around the aged wood.

Without a word, the big man stepped into the alcove and disappeared.

"Up you go, Juno," said one of the Keepers, prodding me forward.

I stepped forward, drawing up my magical senses. Whatever danger was ahead, I wanted to be as prepared as I could.

The sense of overwhelming peace in the church grew stronger, as well as the presence of something magical in the alcove. It flickered with rainbow light—was this the same magic the big man had used to get us here?

"Enough stalling," the same Keeper said, shoving me into the alcove. The last thing I saw before I passed through was Hasebe elbowing the man in the face.

⊰Ω⊱

If I'd been a little girl entering Hogwarts for the first time, it would have left the same impression. The dim corridor I emerged into opened up into a vaulted atrium lined with torches.

Across the room, half a dozen men and women in robes or heavy coats stood on either side of a huge staircase that wouldn't have been out of place in the family manor. Elaborate gilding ran the length of the marble handrails, with what I took to be rune script carved in the centre of each step. The whole place positively shimmered with arcane energies.

The big man was striding toward the staircase as if he owned the place. I followed, taking the opportunity to yank the handkerchief out of my mouth again.

Six pairs of eyes fixed on me as magic stirred in the air. I hadn't a clue how being looked at with farsight felt, if anything at all, but the attention made me uncomfortable. It shouldn't have. The world of privilege I'd grown up in had gotten me used to people staring at me from a young age. Being in the public eye was never an unknown thing, thanks to my status and my father's position in the government.

This, like everything else so far today, had been different. The room around the six figures blurred, shifting colour and texture in odd ways. I almost missed my footing, stopping myself from knocking into the big man's back just in time.

One of the figures, a younger man in a heavy wool coat, had stepped out in front of the big man. He held up a hand, blocking the other's path.

"Who is this, old man?" he said in a precise London accent.

The big man looked over his shoulder. I turned as well to find Hasebe and the contingent of Keepers crowding the stairs behind me. My bodyguard had a bloody lip, but at least his gag was also gone. Two of the Keepers moved to flank me as the tension in the room notched a little higher.

"The disturbance in Johannesburg turned out to be none other than Juno," the big man said in a hushed voice that still echoed through the large room. "I thought the Althing might care to know I'd found her."

The man in the coat startled backward. He regained control quickly, sweeping a lock of brown hair out of his face as he glared. "Damn it, Sturluson, does the word 'security' mean nothing to you? That girl is a criminal and the man has no magic at all!"

"I can hear you," Hasebe said.

My bodyguard's remark earned him a quick glare from the man in the coat before he turned his attention back to Sturluson. "Why didn't you send any warning? Call on the coded landline? Anything but showing up unannounced?"

The big let out a huge sigh. "Do you think I'd fit in a phone booth? Next time, Samuel, I'll follow all your rules and what the hell else. Is the Althing all here?"

The younger man's face was turning red, but he kept his composure as he gritted his teeth and said, "Several of the Low Althing are here. I'll inform Councillor Murphy you're coming. Morgana won't be happy."

"Happiness has nothing to do with it. I'm following my own protocols, boy. Not yours."

"Just go," Samuel snapped, flinging his hands in the air. "Whatever havoc these two cause is on your head."

Sturluson made a rumbling noise in his throat, then started up the stairs again. I put on my most neutral face and followed him, Hasebe close behind. The pressure against my magical senses faded, though not the overwhelming sense of power this place possessed.

So not only are there other magical beings in the world, there's a whole bloody castle full of them. Just how little do I truly know of magic? And who is Morgana? That's the second time someone's mentioned her.

"Cheery reception," I snarked as we followed Sturluson down another narrow hallway. "Do your fellows always greet you like that?"

Behind me, one of the Keepers snickered. Sturluson stopped, turning to glare back at the cluster of green-cloaked figures surrounding us.

"Tolfdir stays with me. The rest of you go. I'll take these two to the Althing's chambers."

The Keepers nodded, dispersing in several directions. One young man nodded and stepped up beside Sturluson, flintlock clutched in both hands.

I saw Hasebe tense as the space around us opened up and shook my head. Anything more than tacit cooperation at this point would be suicide. We were deep in unknown territory with no information and no leverage. The fact that Sturluson had so casually dismissed the rest of our guards made me even more wary of him. That spoke either to his ego... or his confidence that he no longer thought we were of any threat.

I had to think of something, and quickly.

"Surely someone of your power would demand more respect from his peers," I said, trying to appeal to his ego. "You don't seem to be particularly well-liked."

Sturluson rolled his shoulders, his imperious body language softening somewhat.

"I don't do this to make friends, Juno."

I winced, which turned into a shiver as another robed figure passed by us. No wonder wizards wore such heavy robes in all those old stories. This castle was freezing.

"You may think me harsh," he continued, "but many of these young wizards rely too much on their own arrogance. Like must be met with like to maintain order. And I must admit, I do enjoy putting on a show for the younger ones sometimes."

"They seem to know you well," Hasebe commented, falling into step beside me. It seemed he'd also noticed the change in our captor.

"Being the oldest wizard in the world comes with some notoriety," Sturluson said. "Even Morgana seems nothing more than a child to me. I'm not always the most delicate."

As if to illustrate his point, Snorri's broad shoulder brushed against one of the wall sconces as he passed by on the left, tipping the candle it held to the floor with a dull sound and a splatter of wax. The big man let out a breath through his nose, kneeling to replace the candle in its sconce. He touched two fingers to its wick and relit the candle with a brief flicker of power.

"Who is Morgana?" Hasebe asked.

Sturluson glanced from Hasebe to me, narrowing his eyes.

"She can tell you better than I," he said, nodding toward me.

I sighed. "Despite what you seem to think, there's been a terrible mistake. I'm not Juno, nor do I have any idea what the hell is going on here."

The big man stood to his full height, waving a hand in dismissal.

"Morgana will see through your lies. You will not be able to hide from her sight. But there is another choice for you, Juno. Tell me the truth here, and it may go easier for you. I owe you at least that much. You've been worthy prey."

Who the hell is this Juno woman?

I rolled my head side to side, feeling my neck crackle. "I've already told you the truth. Take me to Morgana."

In my periphery I saw Hasebe's eyes sparkle.

"Very well," Sturluson said, shaking his head. "But I warned you."

He turned and started down the hallway again. With the young Keeper bringing up our rear, we were led across an elevated stone walkway to a set of tall wooden doors. I'd been on school trips to castles with doors less impressive than this.

Standing by the door were two more Keepers, still with flintlock pistols in hand.

"Wizard Sturluson," the one on the left said, inclining his head in greeting as we approached. He looked to be in his mid-forties, judging from the salt and pepper in his blonde hair and beard.

"Leif," Snorri replied, reaching out with one hand. The two men gripped each other's forearms, an Old World handshake I'd seen time and again.

"Is this her?" Leif said, gripping his pistol as he eyed Hasebe and I.

"She says she isn't," Sturluson said. "But she was in the right place at the right time. Her guard dog refused to be separated from her."

"You will see how hard I bite if you call me that again," Hasebe said, glaring at the big man.

Sturluson held up a hand. "My apologies. I can see you have a warrior's spirit about you. That alone deserves respect."

Hasebe didn't respond, but his lip curled.

Leif looked at me. "Will your man behave himself?"

"Oh for God's sake," I said, nostrils flaring. "He's my bodyguard, not a bloody German Shepherd."

I shouldn't have said anything, but the tension and fatigue were beginning to get to me. I had already been on edge when we arrived in Johannesburg. The rest of the day had not eased that at all.

"Morgana and the Althing will deal with them both," Sturluson said. "If it turns out she is not lying, which I doubt, further actions will be discussed."

"And if she is?" Leif said, glancing at me again. The suspicion was evident on his face.

"Judgement will be swift."

Leif's grip on his pistol slackened, his hand dropping back to his side.

With a monumental effort, I held my tongue. I needed to try and salvage this situation, gain whatever leverage I could manage.

"Be on your guard," I whispered to Hasebe in Japanese as Leif retreated to his position again.

"I have been," he replied in kind. "These people make a mistake to underestimate me."

My reply was swallowed up in the grinding of wood against stone. One of the big doors trundled open, its base dragging the floor.

Once again, Sturluson walked straight on into the room.

The young Keeper behind us cleared his throat. "Go on in."

I rolled my eyes. *How gracious, treating me like I have a choice.*

Summoning up my most elegant bearing, I followed Sturluson's lead and strode into the audience chamber.

CHAPTER FIVE

THE WORLD BEYOND ME

R ather than the austere, grand courtroom I'd expected after the castle entryway, this Althing's library council room wouldn't have been out of place in the country manor of some Austen love interest.

The library felt warmer, for a start. Its wooden shelves lined with books reminded me of grad school, except I wouldn't have minded reading these books. A large oval table dominated the centre of the cosy library. Three people sat at the opposite end of it from us, peering at the screen of a boxy old laptop.

The first was a young man around my age in a smart navy business suit, his dark hair slicked back. He was bent over the computer, a look of intense concentration on his face as he slid his glasses up the bridge of his nose with one hand. A woman with Asian features sat beside him, clad in a dark robe with a velvet stole thrown over one shoulder.

The third woman was Morgana, I had no doubt. She was younger than I would've expected, only a touch of grey creeping into the roots of her auburn hair. The scarlet robe she wore complimented said hair quite nicely.

I'd kept my magical awareness up as we'd entered the room, which was the reason I was certain of Morgana's identity. She had the same sort of thunderstorm aura of power I'd felt from Sturluson. It stood out even amidst the simmering magic infusing this place. From her sheer power alone, she seemed to be the one in charge.

Morgana glanced up as we entered, revealing a mismatched pair of blue and hazel eyes.

That's odd. Why aren't her eyes golden too?

"This is her, then?" she said, fixing her gaze on me. "The one you've been hunting for months, Wizard Sturluson? The one you cavalierly decided to bring right into the heart of our sanctum?"

The lilt of her Irish accent was harsh rather than musical. That seemed wrong, somehow.

"What harm can Juno be now, surrounded by the wisest and strongest of the Order?" Sturluson replied, gesturing to me.

"We have no idea, despite your best efforts." Morgana put a hand to her forehead. "Snorri, now is not the time to be toying with me."

Snorri... Sturluson?

The name struck a chord in my head. I glanced at the big man. There was no way. It had to have been a coincidence.

He said he was the oldest wizard in the world... surely not. That would make him over eight hundred years old. That's impossible.

"Have you nothing to say in your defence, Juno?"

Morgana's voice brought me out of my head. I let out a sigh, my shoulders slumping.

"As I've already explained, my name is Brooke Gilkeson. I have no idea who this Juno person is, nor do I—"

"Then what were you doing in Johannesburg, hours after a surge of dark sorcery was felt and in the exact location Wizard Sturluson set a trap for Juno?"

It was inevitable. I'd been hoping against hope no one would ask, but there it was. Lying now would only make me seem more suspicious.

"I was looking for someone," I admitted. "A friend of mine disappeared several years ago and I'd heard she was seen in South Africa, specifically near Johannesburg."

The smartly-dressed man closed the lid of the laptop, sitting down in a high-backed chair next to Morgana. The Asian woman shifted in her seat, eyes darting between Morgana and Hasebe.

"Convenient, isn't it?" the young man said, his accent much like Morgana's. "A little too convenient, I think."

"I must agree," Morgana said. "Wizard Sturluson's methods may be unorthodox, but he is rarely wrong. He predicted Juno would be in South Africa, and there you were."

The big man snorted. Hasebe tensed, squeezing his cybernetic fingers so hard they creaked.

I tried to spread my hands, forgetting the shackles. They jerked my arms up short a foot from each other. "How am I to even begin defending myself if you refuse to consider anything I have to say?"

Morgana tilted her head. "This is too grave a matter for us to presume your innocence."

My temper boiled over. "If you're all so bloody high and mighty, surely you've realised there's a way for you to determine whether or not I am what I say I am. Draw the rune."

The young man blinked. "The rune?"

I drew myself up to my full height and fixed him with the arrogant glare I hated using. "Othala. The rune of foundation. As close to divination as you are allowed. Let my very essence prove my intentions, if you doubt my words so much."

My voice changed as I spoke, hardening into the regal tone my father always wanted me to use. It was as though I'd swallowed a whetstone.

Despite my discomfort, my voice seemed to have the desired effect. Sturluson took a step to the side. Morgana raised one thin eyebrow, curiosity etched on her face.

"Defiant, but clinging to the laws of magic. Interesting."

She flicked her left wrist, murmuring a rune word. Magic stirred, sweeping the oval conference table into the air. I almost didn't feel it. The other two wizards skittered back, nearly sending their chairs tumbling to the stone floor.

The table stopped fifteen feet above the floor and hung there as if suspended. I had to give Morgana credit—it was an unexpectedly subtle display of that magic. I'd never read or performed anything indicating this kind of nuance to the Uruz rune than an application of pure, magical force. Moving sand and earth was one thing, but this bordered on telekinesis.

Morgana dusted her hands off, turning back to the others.

"My apologies for the lack of warning, Wizard Murphy, Wizard Hasegawa."

"No need," said the woman in the scarlet stole. "I'm eager to see this as well."

A rune carved into one of the floor stones beneath the table flared to life, bathing its fellows in violet light. The rune was a diamond shape with two prongs extending out from the bottom corners facing me.

Othala, said the part of my mind that knew far more than it should. *Sure enough. Can read as 'homeland,' 'ancestry,' or 'inheritance' depending on the context.*

"Stand on the rune and your truth shall be revealed," Morgana said, her voice also carrying more gravitas.

I locked eyes with Morgana and stepped forward onto the glowing rune. The instant my boots touched it, violet flames burst up and swirled around me. There was no heat to the flames, but they were accompanied by a rush of wind that threatened to finally dislodge my hair from its loose bun. My heart thumped against my ribcage.

Hasebe cried out, lurching forward with shackled hands outstretched.

"Wait!" I said, turning to hold up a hand. "I'm alright. They're not real."

I hoped that would be enough for him.

Something reached out and touched the well of power inside me, filling my body with an icy heat. The old language I sometimes understood whispered in my head.

Before I knew what I was doing, I began to speak.

"Uruz. Sowilo. Laguz. These three are the apex of my power. I am Brooke, daughter of Giles and Maggie, wielder of life and death, Third of the Opened Lock, healer of broken souls."

Still maintaining eye contact with Morgana, I added, *"Test me at your peril."*

I thrust out my left hand, piercing through the cylinder of swirling flames as I drew up my own power. *"Uruz!"*

The illusory violet flames burst apart around me, dissipating in a shockwave through the room that sent a stack of papers fluttering.

Morgana stood in front of me, her hair barely ruffled by the burst of invisible force I'd conjured.

"Very interesting," she said. "Wizard Sturluson, can you tell me which rune was missing from that list?"

"No need to be condescending, Líadin. I'll own my mistake."

The big man approached Hasebe and bowed from the waist, nearly doubling over. "It seems I misjudged you both. I felt the dark working and saw you soon after, so I put two and three together and got four."

Hasegawa, the other woman in the room, did the same.

"Our earnest apologies for the cold welcome," she said in Japanese. "I am journeyman wizard Hanako Hasegawa, member of the Low Althing of the Order of White Wizards. Welcome to Castle Gladsheim," Hasegawa finished in English.

"Express your regret by taking off these shackles," Hasebe said, speaking Japanese. "Then we will discuss restitution."

Sturluson nodded. "I don't speak the language as well as Hanako—eh, Wizard Hasegawa—but I can remove the cuffs."

He gestured and the cuffs melted away into coils of silken rope. Hasebe flexed his wrists, snapping the ropes with a grunt of effort. He turned to glare at Morgana.

"There. Are you satisfied?"

"Not entirely. But I'm certain your employer isn't Juno."

"Just like that?" I said, reeling a little from the experience. "You all were so adamant before, and now you're certain I'm not lying?"

"Can you perform workings with fire?"

I swallowed hard, images of Cari's effortless command of that element flashing through my mind.

"I've never tried, truth be told." I wrinkled my nose. "Fire seemed quite a dangerous element to try and fool with."

"There you have it. The inheritor rune cannot be deceived or manipulated, so it's impossible for you to be lying about that."

"Proof enough for me," Murphy said, adjusting the lapel of his suit jacket. He ran a hand through his hair, slicking it back into place, and cleared his throat.

Sturluson beat him to it.

"Morgana, if you wouldn't mind... I think this girl could be useful to my investigation."

Murphy narrowed his eyes at the big man, but he nodded. "I was about to suggest the same, actually. The Third of this cycle isn't an asset we want to pass over."

"Hold on a tic," I said. "Don't I get any say in this?"

The abrupt shift in tone was more than my overtaxed brain could keep up with. What had I said that was so vindicating? And what did the odd question about fire have to do with it?

My question answered itself. In my fugue state, I'd named off the three runes I seemed to have a knack with. As Morgana had pointed out, the rune representing fire, Kenaz, had not been among them.

Which also meant the one thing they knew for certain about Juno was that she was proficient with that sort of magic.

It can't be Cari. There's no way she's turned into some sort of witch-craft-spewing magical terrorist.

Unfortunately, while my brain was trying to process what had just happened, my mouth had lost all decorum and patience.

"Listen," I said, tapping my foot against the stones for emphasis. "I can appreciate the need for secrecy and talking in riddles. Those are skills I'm quite good at myself. But will someone please explain who you are or what the bloody hell is going on?"

My words hung in the air for a moment, swallowed up by the shelves full of books.

Morgana waved her hand in a dismissive gesture toward me. "Step back, Miss Gilkeson. Once we're seated again Wizard Murphy can explain enough for you to be useful."

I glanced at Hasebe, who shrugged. My cheeks coloured. I hadn't meant to lose control like that. This situation had me more on edge than I'd thought. I had to start reining myself in or we'd never get anywhere.

There was a brief pause as Morgana brought the table back down and we seated ourselves around it.

"The short version, then," she said. "Wizard Murphy, if you would."

Murphy adjusted his glasses again, glancing at each of the others.

"Councillor Aalto is better at this sort of thing than I am," he said. "But I'll do my best. Very, *very* briefly, the currents of magic ebb and flow from this world. Every time they return, there is a span of time where those who are initiated into our Order receive an extra outpouring of magical power. Usually there are nine individuals gifted in this way, but this cycle the special outpourings stopped after just six."

"Initiated... you mean the Drowning?"

That sent a shudder down my back. Eight years ago, during that disastrous summer, I'd drowned in a small pool on an island in the Celtic Sea. The magic had come after that. I'd known it was related, but this was far beyond what I'd ever thought possible.

"Exactly," Murphy said, tilting his head slightly. "All members of our Order are supposed to go through the Drowning. Which means in addition to you, there are two other individuals who entered the Lock after it reopened but before we were aware of it."

"It opened so quietly this time," Hasegawa said, shaking her head. "I'm not surprised we didn't notice it right away."

"Wait, hold on," I said, tapping the wooden table with a finger as a thought clicked. "You mean the pool on that island is some sort of magical nexus?"

"*The* magical nexus," Sturluson said from his seat to my left. "Only those who drink from the Lock and are then drowned can be gifted magic. It's worked that way for over a thousand years."

Murphy frowned, adjusting his glasses. "Well, strictly speaking, that isn't—"

"Briefly, Wizard Murphy," Morgana said, her tone dry but teasing.

"Fair enough," Murphy said. "As Wizard Sturluson has said, the Lock is the source of all magic in the natural world. Any with strong enough potential can receive magic from it, with special outpourings given to the first nine to enter its waters."

"And I was the third of those nine," I said, leaning back in the old wooden chair. That could well be the explanation for Cari's sheer power and Amy's fine control, though even now I wasn't clear on which of them had fallen in first.

Murphy nodded. "The specific effects of the outpouring are not standardised. It's hard to be certain, but that is a real possibility. Any road, the inheritor rune's reaction indicates that you are indeed part of that small group."

"What does this have to do with Juno?" Hasebe said. "Have we not proven enough to you that we are of no harm?"

"It means your employer may be uniquely qualified to aid in bringing her to justice," Morgana said. "Is that what you're getting at, Wizard Sturluson?"

"Exactly." The big man tapped his fingers on the table for emphasis. "She has no training, but I must confess I'm eager to see what sort of inborn surprises the Third Outpouring might have given her. She may be what I need to gain the advantage against our traitorous adversary."

Morgana's lips firmed into a thin line. "That's an enormous risk, Snorri. Can we afford to gamble at such a delicate time?"

"Would you rather Juno gets to this girl first?"

An idea blossomed in my head. Divination was out, but clearly these people had resources and networks that I didn't. Perhaps I could also use them for my own purposes. It certainly took away some of the sting of being treated first like a criminal and now a tool.

"It seems to me," I said, drawing up every scrap of diplomatic skill I possessed, "that there is an opportunity for mutual benefit here. I'm looking for someone, you wish to bring this Juno woman to justice. Our goals may not overlap, but they certainly align. For a price."

Silence filled the room as the four wizards exchanged cryptic glances.

Sturluson chuckled. "Your boldness does you credit, girl. Another reason I want you close by. Just what do you know of magic?"

"Now wait a moment, Sturluson," Murphy said. "That isn't what I had in mind. If she's going to be of any use to us, she must receive some kind of training first."

Sturluson rose from his seat, dusting off his jacket. "It's called on-the-job training. I'm more than powerful enough to compensate, and Aalto's no slouch either."

"My former apprentice may be capable," Morgana said, "but this is still quite an ask."

"I'll be fine," Sturluson said, gesturing to Hasebe and I. "Come on. We have some work to do."

"Hold on," I protested. "We haven't discussed my fee at all."

"Very well," Morgana said, exhaling an exasperated breath. "The Order will owe you a favour, within reason, should you be of aid in this matter."

That left a lot of open loopholes, but it was the best I was likely to get.

"Very well," I said. "I'll hold you to that."

CHAPTER SIX

AALTO AND JUNO

I expected Sturluson to use his magical teleportation again to take us out of the castle, but he instead led us up yet another cramped stone stairway. We emerged onto one of the castle rooftops, where an old RAF helicopter waited with rotors already spinning.

"I didn't know you could fly a helicopter, Sturluson," I shouted above the noise.

"There's a great deal you don't know about me," he replied, winking. "And please, call me Snorri. If we're to be working together I'd prefer the familiar name."

Another green-cloaked Keeper hurried towards us, gesturing toward the helicopter.

"Fueled and ready for your flight to London, sir!"

"Good!" Snorri replied. "Send a message to Councillor Aalto to inform him we'll arrive around high tea."

The young woman nodded, hurrying back the way we'd come. We arranged ourselves in the helicopter, Snorri piloting and the two of us in the back bench seat.

"Why London?" I asked as soon as we'd taken off.

A staticked chuckle came through the earphones as Snorri shook his head.

"I was going to wait til we convened with Aalto, but very well. Juno has been breaking into secret wizard storehouses located around the world. It's not clear if she's looking for something or just wants to cause trouble, but she's certainly doing the latter. The next one on our list to check is in London."

"Is there no pattern?" Hasebe asked. "No common thread between items?"

"Most of what she's taken are ritual pieces that could be used for anything—an enchanted athame, magically purified salt, those sorts of things." Snorri hunched his shoulders forward. "But I must be honest. This one is different. I can sense it."

"As you sensed Juno in South Africa?"

I shot my bodyguard a look, but he was right. Snorri had been wrong in that case. It had worked out for us, but if he got something wrong again...

"How exactly are you able to sense things of that nature?" I asked before Snorri could reply. "I thought divination was an accursed art that drew down the wrath of God or some such."

"It is, but that's not what I've done." Snorri glanced over his shoulder at me. "If I worked for an ordinary government organisation my role would be as a detective, more specifically a profiler. I've always had a knack for reading people and being able to predict their movements."

"I repeat myself," Hasebe said, his eyes narrowing. "Clearly you were wrong to assume she was Juno in Johannesburg."

"I was... a bit hasty in my reading of the situation. My apologies, little wizard," Snorri added, glancing at me again. "I will take greater care in the future."

I nodded. "Then permit me another question. Are you... *that* Snorri Sturluson?"

He raised an eyebrow. "How do you mean?"

My cheeks flushed. "It sounds bloody stupid, but there's only one man I've ever heard of by that name. Taken together with your statement that you're the oldest wizard in the world, and..."

My earphones shook as Snorri's belly laugh rumbled through the speakers.

"I take your meaning now! Yes, little one. I am that Snorri Sturluson, compiler and author of the *Prose Edda* and the *Heimskringla*, among others."

There was a twinkle in his eye as he spoke. "Wish I'd kept up on that one, to be honest. Iceland doesn't have kings anymore, but there are still many out there who would kill for those stories."

I had no idea what the *Heimskringla* was, but the fact he was claiming to be a man who'd been writing books almost eight centuries ago was still a bit much.

"That is impossible," Hasebe said. "What evidence do you have to support your claim?"

"The proof of my existence, among other things. The effect of magic on a wizard's body serves to slow down its decay, much like the fabled apples of Idunn. Morgana herself was only born in 1887."

"Right, then." *Only* born in 1887. That was still over a century beyond me. Everything was relative, I supposed.

I sat back in my seat, my mind churning with questions and speculation. It was a great deal to take in all at once. And I was so knackered...

⊰⋔⊱

LONDON, UNITED KINGDOM

I woke up as the helicopter jolted, alert for danger or something else going wrong today. I was greeted instead by a familiar cityscape.

"Not the most idyllic part of London, Battersea," I commented, stretching as we disembarked the helicopter. "But it's good to be back."

We took a cab, one with a human driver, and after crossing Blackfriars Bridge passed into the historic part of London. Fleet Street looked as it always did, people bustling about their business. The scents of old paper and ink invaded my nose, though I couldn't actually smell them from inside the cab.

"Where are we going?" Hasebe asked. "I would not expect a secret storehouse to be in the heart of London."

"I expect that's why it's there," I said, the sight and scenery of my city putting me at ease. We weren't far from my flat in Knightsbridge, either. For a moment I considered asking Snorri to let us out so I could pop home for a change of clothes. Hasebe would have appreciated the opportunity to gear up, I knew—we'd left all our gear and equipment in the penthouse in Johannesburg.

I pulled my phone out of my pocket to find it unresponsive. Bloody battery had died again, then. That was the third one this month.

"I don't know about you," Snorri said as our cab pulled alongside the walk, "but I could use a drink."

Hasebe helped me out of the backseat. I straightened up to find myself looking at a familiar chequered glass shopfront. In the middle of the window, antique-looking lettering proclaimed our destination to be The Old Bell Tavern.

"This time of day?" I said as we made our way inside. "It'll be packed."

"We won't be staying long," Snorri said, turning sideways to move through the crowd.

The pub was indeed crowded, but we managed to find our way to a small circular table by the front windowpane. A young man already seated there looked up as we approached.

"Have you been waiting long, Aalto?' Snorri said, stopping in front of the man with a broad grin.

Unlike every other wizard we'd met so far, this one blended right in with my world. His hair was dyed a striking navy blue that complimented the dark leather jacket he wore over his street clothes. He didn't look a day over twenty-seven, if I had to guess.

The man I presumed to be Aalto sipped at his gin and tonic, dark eyes staring up at Snorri. From there his gaze drifted downward, meeting my eyes.

His body language changed in an instant, sitting straight up in his seat as his fingers clamped around his glass. I felt his eyes boring into me, as though he were trying to peer into my soul. He broke the uncomfortable silence a moment later.

"Well then. You've picked up company."

His voice carried a northern brogue, gentle but clearly present.

"Finn Aalto, this is Brooke and Hasebe," Snorri said, gesturing to each of us in turn. "Brooke, Hasebe, this is my partner for my investigation."

Aalto raised his glass to me before downing the rest in one swallow. "Right then. I've been people-watching for the last two hours. Let's go."

He slapped a pair of bills on the table and stood, shuffling past us toward the door.

What the hell was that?

The other wizards had been short, but nothing close to that sort of interaction once they'd found out I wasn't Juno. Why did I get the feeling Aalto didn't like me?

"Charming," Hasebe said.

Snorri glanced from Aalto's retreating form to me, one eyebrow raised. "I suppose we'd best be off."

Retracing our steps through the crowded pub, we retreated back to the street.

Aalto glanced over and nodded as we emerged. "I assume you've been brought up to speed?"

"No," Hasebe said, "but here we are. Where are we going?"

Aalto shot an indecipherable look at Snorri, then cocked his thumb toward Bride Street. "Fancy a walk to a church?"

"What sort of fascination do you people have for churches?" I said, shaking my head as we started down the street.

"Churches were an easy way to stay inconspicuous five hundred years ago," Sn0rri replied, stroking his beard. "Nothing against the Christians, mind. It's just that the bad wizards who go crazy and start doing witchcraft and killing people and kidnapping children give the more noble-intentioned among us a bad name. Hard for anyone to believe you're an evil, bloodthirsty *seidhkona* if they see you listening to the rector's sermon every Sunday."

Yet again with these people, there seemed to be some historical context I was missing. My gift was at least kind enough to remind me again what *'seidhkona'* meant. In the Old Icelandic, it meant 'sorcery-woman.'

Or more accurately, 'witch.' The bad kind of magic wielders.

"Things changed a lot in the Middle Ages," Aalto added. "Especially after the Inquisition."

"Apparently," I said. "What's so special about Saint Bride's, anyhow? I assume that's where we're heading. It's been burned down and rebuilt so many times I'd think it would be difficult to keep anything at all hidden there."

"We did almost lose the storehouse during the Blitz bombing in the 40's. The storehouse is in a part of the crypt that was never excavated." Aalto shrugged. "At least, that's the story. I wasn't there."

"Are there countermeasures we should be concerned with?" Hasebe asked. "Surely a group of such paranoid foxes would set traps for their burrow."

"No," Aalto said, smirking at Hasebe. "I've been given an access pendant to disarm the magical defences and wards. Still wouldn't hurt to be on guard, just in case."

"I wouldn't be anything else," my bodyguard replied. From a younger man it might have sounded overly macho. Hasebe made it into a simple statement of fact.

≪⋔≫

Saint Bride's Church hadn't changed much from when I'd visited as a little girl. For my mother's benefit, we'd made a pretense of attending a weekly service here. That had lasted only through the summer of my sixth birthday, but even as an adult there was something oddly compelling about the tenets of faith I drifted back to from time to time.

Twenty years' passage meant the sanctuary felt even smaller as the four of us entered it, our footsteps echoing off the black and white tiles. The beautiful curved ceilings were the same, though, still sporting their elaborate gold trimming.

Aalto led us past the polished wooden pews to a back stairway, descending fifteen feet below the ground. He paused in front of the door at the bottom of the stairs, holding up a metal key. Then his expression froze in a neutral mask. The blue-haired man pushed the door with two fingers, as if trying to open it without the key.

The door creaked open a few inches, scattering dust as it did.

Hasebe held up his Cobalt, making eye contact with Aalto. The two men nodded at each other before Aalto pushed the door open and slipped into the crypt.

I hadn't visited the crypt as a child, but it was sort of famous. Saint Bride's crypt had been built on the remains of at least six other churches, including one dating back to the Roman era.

"How far down will we need to go?" I whispered, following behind Hasebe.

Snorri, sideways behind me on yet another narrow staircase, bumped his head into the door's frame. He swore softly in a language I didn't recognize.

"We'll have to go down a level or two," he said. "I may not fit down these stairs."

"Quiet!" Hasebe hissed. "We are already compromised here. Do not make it worse."

I reached under my blazer, gripping the butt of the taser handgun Snorri had returned to me. It would have to do.

Aalto stopped, turning to face us. He pointed at his mouth, then his forehead, raising an eyebrow in question. I frowned, not quite sure what he was asking.

Oh! Does he mean... of course. I should've known

He was asking for permission to set up magical telepathy—the same kind I'd used long ago, at a guess. I nodded, waving a hand to grab Hasebe's attention. I mimicked Aalto's first two motions, then ended with an affirmative nod of my head. Hasebe's gaze flicked between the two of us before his jaw set, though a question remained in his eyes.

Aalto pulled a Sharpie from his jacket pocket and held out his right hand palm down. On the back of his hand he drew a rune that looked like an uppercase 'F' with its tines bent down, inscribing the same symbol on each of our hands in turn.

Ansuz, said my mind. *The rune of communication. Of course that's what we did.*

"You've done this before?" Aalto's voice echoed in my head.

Hasebe startled back, knocking into me. His thought-voice came through the link, a string of Japanese so fast I couldn't make it out.

"It's all right, Hasebe," I projected. *"This is a form of instant communication that won't give us away. Simply think the words you want to say. The magic will do the rest."*

"I was wondering when we'd finally get a taste of your power," Aalto's voice said. *"You have done this before."*

"She's the Third of this cycle, Aalto," Snorri's voice said. *"Not a battle-mage or the like, but impressive for someone with no training."*

"What a wonder," Hasebe said through the link. *"I am no* yokai, *yet I may still speak in my thoughts this way."*

"I set up the bind-rune," Aalto said, *"so my magic and those marks are sustaining the communication link. Normal people are able to use it, and this is more efficient than me maintaining the link this whole time."*

"Good, good," Snorri said. *"I'll stay behind you three. Make sure she can't escape."*

"Well she certainly won't be sneaking around you up these stairs, that's for sure."

Snorri chuckled as Aalto started down the stairs again. He kept four or five paces ahead of Hasebe, hugging one side of the room. My bodyguard seemed to sense this, moving to the other side. I shifted that way as well, keeping behind Hasebe.

This level of the crypt was the museum floor, plaques and display pieces arranged artfully around the room. We ignored all of it and proceeded to a metal door in the rear of the room. Its handle had been melted away, leaving this door ajar as well.

"Let's not waste time," I said. *"Juno could very well be trying to escape, if she hasn't already."*

"There's only one way out," Aalto said, *"and it's through this door. Every other avenue is warded against."*

"That is worse," Hasebe said, his voice much louder than before.

"Gently, Hasebe," I said, biting my lip to stifle a cry of pain. *"It takes less than you think to send your thoughts."*

"You are missing my point," my bodyguard replied, though his mental voice softened. *"A cornered fox will fight to its death. If the Juno woman is truly there, this is her high noon. She has nothing to lose."*

"Then we'll have to strike first," Aalto said. *"Breaching the door in three, two—"*

He pulled open the door and darted into the room beyond.

"—one!"

Hasebe took a step forward, then froze as a thin lance of fire streaked past him. It missed me by a hair and splashed against the stone wall to our left. My bodyguard crouched, raising his arms in a shooting stance before firing three shots into the vault room.

"Watch the shelves!" Aalto's thought-voice said. From inside the room came the sounds of a scuffle, followed by something crashing to the floor.

Drawing the little handgun, I called up my power and peeked around the corner into the vault.

It was a stone room lit by torches burning a bright violet colour, maybe half again as big as the room we were currently in. Bookshelves lined one wall, and there was a heavy wooden table of a similar style to the one in Castle Gladsheim in the centre of the room. Aalto lay across its wreckage, the table broken in half where he'd apparently been thrown against it.

The woman standing over him wore a charcoal grey combat jumpsuit. Had it not been for the hood and helmet beneath, she could have been any government's special agent. In one hand she clutched a book bound in dark leathers. Drawing a short sword with her other hand, the masked woman inverted it and plunged it towards Aalto's prone chest.

I snapped off three buzzing shots into the vault, ears protesting with each retort. I'd left my combat earplugs in the Johannesburg hotel, too.

And my damn knives. Those would be quite helpful. Again.

The woman's trajectory changed from stabbing down to throwing herself prone next to Aalto, sword clattering on the stone floor. Hasebe took the opportunity to position himself in the doorway, gun trained on the woman.

"Don't move!" he barked. "You are outnumbered."

"And you're outgunned, pretty boy," the woman said, a modulator in her helmet imparting a buzzing rumble to her words. *"Uruz!"*

She flung out her left hand, dust and splinters stirring as a wave of invisible force smashed into Hasebe. My bodyguard was thrown backwards, almost taking me with him. I ducked just in time but still got some pebbles in my face for all the trouble.

There was a snapping crack and a hiss. Scarlet smoke billowed out of the room, obscuring everything in the crypt we stood in. Someone rushed past me in the smoke, almost knocking me to the ground. The woman, I guessed. Against my better judgement, I turned and raced after her, bouncing off display pedestals and walls I couldn't see.

Sure enough, when I emerged from the crypt stairwell, she was almost out the front doors of Saint Bride's, still clutching the book.

I paused just inside the sanctuary.

She's far more powerful than I expected, and Hasebe's stunned. I should wait.

But if she gets away, we get even less of a chance to stop her, my more reckless side thought.

"Stay where you are," Aalto's voice came through the link. That meant he wasn't dead, but I hadn't known a thought could be so jumbled. *"I'm almost there."*

The roar of a small engine cut through the city ambiance.

"No time," I sent. *"She's got a bike."*

CHAPTER SEVEN

PURSUIT

I dashed outside to see the woman, still trailing red smoke, rocket past down the street on a motorcycle.

Snapping my little gun up, I fired off the clip's last two shots, aiming for the tyres of her bike. Sparks flew up from the street as the shots went wide.

Only then did it cross my mind that gunshots would attract attention. I swore, glancing around for my next move.

Snorri burst out of the church as though it were on fire. He dropped to one knee on the walk next to me, drawing a circle around him with the chalk.

"Ehwaz!" he thundered, slamming a hand down on the sidewalk.

There was a pulse of teal light that shimmered up from the circle's radius. The air itself rippled, and in the circle beside Snorri was a monstrous, translucent bear. I hadn't thought anything could make the big man look small. This animal managed it.

Without a word, Snorri leapt onto the creature's back, sending out puffs of the same teal light. The bear leapt over a parked car, landing in the centre of the road. Someone nearby screamed.

"Let's go!" Snorri bellowed, waving me up.

"What the hell is this?" I said, shoving the handgun in my blazer pocket.

"*Fylgja,*" the big man said, pulling me onto the bear's back with one hand. "It's the only chance we have to catch her. Hyah!"

He dug in his heels, spurring the bear on. It unleashed a mighty roar and lunged down Fleet Street in the direction the woman had gone. Once it got going, the creature made better speed than I'd thought it could, dodging around cars like they weren't there. Several honked in protest, the sound dopplering past as the bear ran.

"Are the others alright?" I called.

"Ask them yourself," Snorri said, tapping his forehead. "The rune is still active."

"*Hasebe?*" I called out with my power. "*Status update.*"

"*I am winded, but I will live,*" his voice came back. "*Is the big* yokai *with you?*"

"*Yes,*" I said. "*We're in pursuit of that woman.*"

"*We'll be there as soon as I've hotwired this car,*" Aalto's voice said.

A twinge of envy shot through me. I'd always wanted to learn to hotwire a car.

"There!" Snorri said, pointing. I looked up to see the woman jump a divider, weaving in between lanes against traffic.

"Off the street!" I snapped. "I don't want to find out what happens when a ghost bear gets hit by a bus."

Snorri shifted his weight, forcing the bear up onto the pavement as we raced past the Savoy. I'd never stayed there, but its decades-old façade radiated high class even in the split second we passed it.

"Is that Juno?" I asked.

"Finn would be the one to tell you. It's a good bet."

"*Was that Juno?*" I asked in the link. "*Did she get anything?*"

"I was a bit busy getting tossed around," Aalto replied. *"I'm more concerned by the fact she keeps finding these allegedly secret places."*

"You have a traitor in your ranks," Hasebe said. *"Perhaps this was years in the planning."*

"It would be far simpler to decide that if we could work out who she was," Aalto said.

"I'm doing what I can," Snorri said, his thought-voice strained. It was a long conversation considering the circumstances. At the speed of thought, however, it took barely a few seconds.

The bear leapt over a crosswalk, landing on the opposite side of the street with a jolt. I caught a flicker of our reflection in a passing shop window. We were wrapped in the illusion of a sporty yellow Arch motorbike. That explained why no one had panicked about the bear, at least.

"We can still see her," I said. *"If we can make up any distance we might catch her."*

"En route," Aalto said. *"Where are you?"*

"Making for Saint James' Park, it looks like. We're less than two minutes from the Thames. She could escape either way."

"We must hurry!" Snorri said, spurring the bear again. It howled, but did begin to move faster. A police siren kicked on somewhere behind us.

"Snorri, you never answered my question!" I said. "Why are we riding a Norse guardian spirit? How did you do that?"

"Old magic, not workings you see much these days," he called back. "Supposed to take longer to bring these beasties over, but I know where they live in the Wilds."

I would have inquired further, but the bear made another almighty leap that brought us within ten feet of Juno. The masked woman glanced over her shoulder, did a double take, then loosed another thin lance of fire back at us. Her shot went wide, striking a streetlamp as we galloped past it. The firebolt passed through the holographic light, shorting it out in a burst of sparks.

I grabbed my taser handgun again, hit the switch on the grip's side to swap clips, and sighted on Juno again. My aim was ruined by a self-driving lorry swerving out of our way. Our bear mount leapt over it, almost cracking my head on the bottom of the Admiralty Arch.

I considered snarking at Snorri about staying incognito but decided against it. We had almost caught up to Juno, after all.

A second police siren made me reconsider. This one was far closer.

The bear stayed close to Juno's bike for another few blocks, following her through a sharp left turn that took us past St. James' Park. The smells of damp earth and blooming flowers filled my nose as we passed the lake. Juno and I continued trading magic and bullets, both swerving between lanes. My only goal was to shoot out her tyres, but she seemed to know just when to dodge.

The roar of another motorcycle filled my ears as the police sirens grew louder. We were running out of grace before they started shooting too.

Snorri's attention seemed to be occupied with wrangling the *fylgja*, keeping the massive bear at pace. Juno darted and wove around other vehicles and traffic, making a third sharp left towards Big Ben. Her skills were impressive, in a stupid, daredevil sort of way. As the old clock towered over us, maintenance drones buzzing around its peak like flies, the three of us reached Westminster Bridge over the Thames.

"Aalto?" I sent. *"What's your location?"*

"Right in front of you."

I glanced up, looking side to side. Juno was still ahead of us, but approaching from the opposite direction was a black and green Mini

Cooper with the driver's side window broken out. Aalto sat behind the wheel, with Hasebe perched in the passenger seat.

"Stand ready," Hasebe said.

"Ready for what?"

By the time I'd gotten the thought out, the Mini Cooper's tyres squealed on the pavement, sending up smoke as the small car geared up and drove straight at Juno's bike.

"Hasebe!" I said, my grip tightening on Snorri.

My bodyguard popped his gun hand out the open window and fired two shots squarely into Juno's front tire. The bike lurched, only for the Mini Cooper to smash headlong into it. Juno's forward momentum took her over the handlebars, smashing the car's windscreen before tumbling over the car's roof.

The ghost bear disappeared from under Snorri and I. He was ready for it, landing on his feet. I stumbled, catching myself on the bridge's stone railing.

Aalto and Hasebe jumped out of the car, the latter training his gun on something behind the car's boot. Two police cars and a motorcycle approached from the other side of the bridge, screeching to a stop twenty yards from us.

"Stay down, Juno," Aalto said. "Hand over what you've stolen and this will go easier for you."

A rattling cough, garbled by the helmet's speaker, came through. "Not happening. This is too important."

"Stealing from your former colleagues is not a way to make you any friends," Hasebe said.

Juno chuckled, the sound more menacing paired with the synthesiser. "Sure. Keep thinking that. Friends are overrated anyway."

I was making my way towards them when that electric sensation of power stirred in the air again. This wasn't quite the thunderstorm of Snorri or Morgana, but it wasn't far off.

"Uruz!"

With an explosive showering of safety glass, the damaged Mini Cooper flipped up and over, crashing to the ground where Snorri and I had been a moment before. A flash of scarlet and grey was the only warning I had as Juno leapt to her feet, shoved me aside, and vaulted the stone railing.

"Wait!" I shouted. "That fall will kill you!"

I ran to the railing, looking over just in time to see the masked woman's descent slow to a crawl before she slipped gracefully into the Thames.

Damn... my one lead, blown. What am I to do now?

"Right, stop there!" a rough voice shouted over a PA speaker. "None of you move!"

I raised my hands, careful not to move too quickly as I locked eyes with Hasebe, tilted my head to the left, and nodded. His chin dipped in an almost imperceptible nod. The revolver in his hands had vanished.

"What the hell is all this?" I said, putting on my most arrogant face and voice as the policemen approached. I pictured my father at his most upset. It helped more than I liked.

"That's the question we ought to be asking you," the nearest officer said, approaching and pointing an accusatory finger at me. "You could've killed someone driving like that!"

"Let's see some licence and registration," the other female officer said, extending a hand toward me.

Hasebe reached into his pocket and presented the officer a laminated card and a small roll of e-paper.

"Not yours. Hers."

"You have no reason to detain me," I said. "I know my rights."

"Rights bloody nothing. If you haven t got a licence we're going to have—"

"Do you know who my father is?" I glared at the male officer. "Giles Corbyn. He's a very wealthy man who could make your life very troublesome."

"Are you threatening an officer of the law?" the female cop said, her hand moving to the nightstick on her belt.

"I'm merely stating facts. It would be in your best interest to take note of them."

She opened her mouth to say something, but the male officer held out a hand. "Wait a tic. Your old man is Giles Corbyn? Member of Parliament Lord Giles Corbyn?"

"You heard me," I said. "I won't repeat myself."

"My deepest apologies on behalf of my employer," Hasebe said, offering a formal bow to the two officers. "I tried to prevent her from doing anything foolish, but she insisted she could handle the vehicle under my supervision."

He reached into his blazer pocket and pulled out a sheaf of cash. "Will five thousand pounds cover the damages?"

The two officers exchanged glances. The male cop had turned a shade or two paler, sweat visibly breaking out on his forehead.

"Er... yes," he said, reaching out for the money. "We'll take this in and hold it til insurance can be contacted. Should be sufficient for any fines or tickets we'd cite you for, too."

"See that it is," I said, turning on a heel. I glanced over my shoulder to add, "And should any further action be taken against me, rest assured you'll hear from my solicitors. Plural."

The female officer began to protest, but the other shushed her.

"It's more trouble than it'll be worth. Trust me. She's already paid for herself. Let it be."

Hasebe exchanged a final goodbye with the two officers and had soon caught up with me.

"You play the part well," he said.

"I hate having to do that," I said, bile rising in my throat. "Eugh. I feel as though I need a shower."

"We need to find the others first," Hasebe said. "Aalto and Sturluson have vanished."

"Of course they have. They might have actually been useful in that situation." I sighed. "Nothing for it but to—"

"Miss Gilkeson?" Snorri's voice floated into my head. I'd forgotten about the magical link.

"Scared off by the constabulary, were we?" I sent. I wasn't in a mood to be charitable.

"You seemed to have the situation handled. We are five blocks past Big Ben, on the other side of the bridge. There's a small cafe where we can talk."

I shook my head, turning to Hasebe. "Did you get that?"

My bodyguard nodded. "If we were trying to make a good impression on the wizards, we may have failed."

"Probably. We'd better see how pear-shaped this is going to go."

CHAPTER EIGHT

ULTIMATUM

I f the shouting on the other end of the courtesy phone was any indication, Aalto's peers had not taken the news of the raid well.

"I am well aware of the consequences, John," Aalto snapped. "Do you think I wanted to steal a car and go on a high-speed chase through London? She almost flipped the car on us!"

I exchanged a glance with Hasebe. We'd seen some incredible things done with magic in my youth. It wasn't much of a stretch to think an invisible force that could smash a man into the wall could also turn a car end over end.

Aalto's conversation went on, still audible from where we stood just outside the courtesy booth. Said booths were supposed to have privacy filters, but the software had malfunctioned as soon as he'd stepped inside.

Snorri's brow was furrowed, giving the impression of an ancient Viking despite his tailored suit.

"Why is Aalto making such a fuss over the car?" I asked. "Surely that's not an uncommon feat with magic."

"Magic isn't dissimilar to physics," Snorri replied. "It takes energy to move things. Could you lift a car with your bare hands?"

"Of course not."

"Performing magic is much the same. We didn't know it eight centuries ago, but all we wizards are doing is applying energy to the world in different ways."

"How does that relate to Juno flipping over a Mini Cooper?" I asked. "Unless you're suggesting she'd have to have an immense amount of magical strength to perform a feat of physical strength such as that."

My heart skipped a beat.

"Hellfire," I swore. "Who is this woman?"

Hasebe shot me a look. I returned it with frosty interest.

"If Cari wanted to lay low and not be found, she wouldn't be travelling the globe breaking into secret wizard vaults."

"Cari?" Snorri asked, tilting his head. "Who is she?"

I gnawed on my lower lip. Telling Snorri the full truth now was likely to paint a target on my friend's back, regardless of whether or not she was guilty. There was no way Juno could be Cari, but I didn't have time to explain to Snorri or Aalto why that was the case. I needed their help to find her, not execute her.

"An old friend who made a mistake," I said after a moment. "She's unwell and needs my help. I've been trying to find her for over two years."

"I'm sorry to hear that," Snorri said. He put a hand on my shoulder, fingers reaching halfway down my bicep. "I've lost many friends over the years. Saved a few, but lost more."

"If you're trying to reassure me, it's not working."

"Would that I could do more," Snorri said. "There might be some in the Wilds who could tell you where she is, but dealing with them is more dangerous than beneficial."

"Blast it, Sturluson, you're holding out on me again," I said. "What are the Wilds?"

A sharp curse in Gaelic and the slamming of a plastic phone receiver cut his reply short. I looked up as Aalto stormed out of the phone box, golden irises ablaze. The courtesy phone died with a puff of smoke, followed by a persistent, electronic whine.

"Walk with me, Brooke," he said. "I need a moment of your time."

I turned to Hasebe. "There's an Everdenes 'round the corner. Give me five minutes."

"Two," Hasebe said. "Not a second more."

"Very well," I said, tipping my head as I hurried to catch up with Aalto.

"Damn Murphy and his weasel tongue," the blue-haired man said, his brogue thicker than normal.

"That didn't sound like it went well," I said.

"There's an understatement."

While it was stating the obvious, one of the first points to building rapport with my counselling clients was to validate their feelings. I suspected the same was true here.

"Buy you a coffee and we can talk?" I offered.

Aalto let out a long exhale through his nose. "Honestly, that sounds great."

Neither of us said another word til we'd gotten our coffees and sat down at one of the little patio tables outside the cafe.

"John is, shall we say, extremely irritated that Juno escaped," Aalto said, sipping his drink. "Morgana agrees with him, but not for the reason you'd think."

"Did we draw too much attention trying to chase her down?"

Aalto's expression didn't change, but his eyes began fading to their normal grey-green.

"That's not the concern. It's the book she got away with. That's Morgana le Fay's grimoire."

"Hold on a tic—she's real?"

It dawned on me as soon as I'd said it that Snorri had called Morgana 'Líadin' at the council meeting.

Morgana isn't a name anymore—it's a title. After the first one.

"Morgana le Fay founded our order," Aalto said, sipping his coffee. "Nine hundred years ago or so. United all the feuding wizards under one banner, mostly by being scarier and more powerful than anybody in the room."

"Seems to have worked, if you're still around almost a millennium later." I leaned back in my chair. "What was in the book?"

"Le Fay's personal research and observations about magic. Which works out to be some of the most powerful and esoteric spells ever created. Including certain runelore and ritual workings that could quite literally shatter reality."

I snorted. "What, and somebody just left it lying on a shelf in a church crypt? No protection or guards or anything?"

Aalto rolled his eyes. "That's what I said. Apparently hiding the thing in plain sight was the brilliant master plan. That might've worked in 1726, but I'd have locked the damn thing away in a Swiss vault if I had any say in it."

I was beginning to like the blue-haired wizard.

"It was written in code, so that'll slow her down some," Aalto continued. "That is, unless she knows where the cipher is."

"Let me guess, stowed away on someone's bookshelf next to gran's recipe for chocolate biscuits?"

"Oslo, actually. There's a vault there too. Snorri's being sent to check on it quick as he can manage. I have my own assignment elsewhere."

"What about Hasebe and I?" I asked, certain I wouldn't like the answer.

Aalto's jaw clenched as he set his cup down on the table. It wasn't shaped quite right anymore.

"I was told to instruct you and Hasebe to meet up with someone local who can return you to Reykjavik."

"Well," I said, dry as the desert. "Am I to be sworn to secrecy, or executed?"

"It's... worse than that, actually. The Keepers will detain you and skirt the line between magic and witchcraft by removing your memories of these events. That's the nuclear option, more or less. There's a chance it could even make you forget your magic."

"You know, I'm not coming away with a very positive impression of your colleagues."

My words were glib, but I felt my heart's pace quicken.

I didn't even know it was possible to forget one's magic... would they really do that over a simple failure?

Again, my question answered itself. This wasn't just a simple failure—it was a catastrophic one, which Aalto's Althing seemed intent to blame on me.

"Look, for what it's worth, I agree with you," Aalto said. "And... I've got an ace, something that might get you out of trouble if it comes to that. I might be able to persuade Lía to initiate you into the Order instead, to preserve secrecy or some such."

I gnawed at my lip. Neither option was anywhere close to a good outcome, but only one meant I wouldn't lose my magic.

Still...

"I'm not keen on being inducted into a group that seems to only see me as a tool, or something to be used," I said.

"I... that's entirely fair," Aalto said. "In that case, let me offer you an olive branch, of sorts."

He cleared his throat before leaning back in his chair.

"I'm not supposed to tell you that a man named Nicolás de la Cruz is an arcane blacksmith living in San Diego, California. In no way do you know that I'm to meet with him at his shop tomorrow night to discuss a powerful ritual contained in le Fay's journal that would require his craftsmanship to facilitate."

"I see," I said. I took a long drink, giving myself space to digest the information I hadn't been given. "Well, if you're trying to give me enough rope to hang myself, that's an excellent start. We both know I can't just let this drop."

"You strike me as the sort of woman who doesn't care for being left out of the loop, either," Aalto said. "I've told you nothing. You do with that what you wish."

"I've spent my whole life around a man who made it his business to tell me how far I fell short for not knowing things I was never told." The cup crinkled as my fingers tightened on it. "My flat in Knightsbridge is the only reason I haven't lost my mind yet."

"So you're from London, then?" Aalto asked, stirring another cream into his coffee.

"I was born in Bristol," I said, not sure quite how much to share with a man I'd known for less than two hours. "Lived there for nearly half my life, went to uni and grad school in New York. My best friend was American."

"Was?"

Damn it all. I hadn't meant to refer to Cari in the past tense.

"You know, for someone wanting to keep me in the loop, you've left out any details about yourself that might be interesting," I countered.

To my surprise, Aalto didn't seem upset. He ran the fingers of one hand through his hair, a chagrined smile on his face.

"That's fair. My first name is Finn. I'm twenty-eight, my parents met on holiday in Amsterdam, and Lía still doesn't understand why I enjoy heavy metal."

I chuckled. "Dad's the same way. His musical tastes died when he was a child. In the seventies."

"Ouch."

"Mum said it was the final straw that moved us to Cardiff ten years back," I said.

I'd meant the words to be lighthearted, but even as I said them I heard the old bitterness in my voice. I'd never forgiven my father for his shady dealings, or for tearing apart my family because of his connections.

"Cardiff has some nice spots," Aalto said, breaking the tense silence that had settled over the table.

I waved a hand. "Sorry. No need to dig into old graves better left unturned."

"You don't have much of a social life, do you?"

The bluntness of his question almost got a sharp response out of me. I held my tongue just enough to say. "I have a rather complicated history with friends and social peers."

Before he could say anything else, I pressed on. "Why are you being so forthcoming about all your wizard secrets? That seems somewhat countercultural, if your peers are any indication."

"Some of them have lived a century or two," Aalto said, not missing a beat. If he was embarrassed at his line of questioning, he covered it well. "When you've been in a world so removed for so long, it gets hard to talk to people outside it. You forget that others don't know all the things you do. And as I said, keeping you out of the loop seems unwise."

"Then tell me this," I said. "Why are you keeping me informed if I'm only a liability? Snorri's power speaks for itself, you seem to have a good grasp of Hasebe's abilities..." I trailed off. "All I have is knowledge with no context and the ability to heal myself, but that's hardly useful for anyone else."

"First off, that sort of life magic has a lot of benefits for your lifespan," Aalto said. "Thirty years from now, you'll still look like a woman in her mid-twenties. Cosmetic companies would kill for that kind of intel."

"Fair point, I'll concede that one."

"Second," he went on, "do you know which runes you're attuned to?"

"Uruz, Laguz, and Sowilo, if the inheritor rune is to be believed. Only the latter one has had any kind of impressive result."

"I've been told that when a wizard is Drowned, at least two runes will choose him or her. It's more common to have a stronger affinity for something like healing or enchantment or evocation, though not all three."

"What's your point?" I asked, downing the last of my coffee.

"My point is that you can evocate better than you probably think you can. You just need some sort of tool to focus those energies of death magic."

"What, like a magic wand?" I mimed casting a spell, snapping my wrist as though I were levitating a feather. "Swish, then flick!"

Aalto smirked. "Maybe, if it helps. A certain arcane blacksmith I know may be able to direct you to the right tool. He lives in San Diego, as a matter of fact. Runs a shop called 'God's Hammer Metalworks.'"

The man was clever, I had to give him that much. He couldn't invite me along with him, the Althing would more or less forbid that. But the blue-haired wizard had given me just enough information to find his next destination and a plausible reason for going there.

If only I didn't have a bad feeling about it.

Why was this man, who I barely knew from Adam, being so open with his secrets? It was an attitude I respected to be sure, in light of my teenaged campaign against my father as an internal reformist. And he was cute, in a James Dean kind of way.

That thought stopped me cold.

When was the last time I even noticed a man my own age?

I was glad Aalto had taken it on himself to dispose of our cardboard coffee cups. It prevented him from seeing the flush of colour that rose on my cheeks. Perhaps Hasebe was right—I'd not really been acting my age much these past few years.

Aalto straightened his coat as he returned to our table. He'd seemed to regain some of his earlier attitude. "Well, Miss Gilkeson, it was nice meeting you and your associate. If we ever cross paths again, drinks are on me."

"I appreciate the generosity, Mister Aalto," I said, putting all the gravitas I'd learned over the last twenty years into the words. "Thank you for your time, and your total lack of useful information."

The blue-haired man grinned back at me and continued off down the street, disappearing around the corner. I sat at the table, taking in the old city's ambiance as I weighed our options. Hasebe wouldn't care for either one, but he would follow my lead.

Joining up with the White Order was certainly the simplest way out of our situation, but that came with its own set of annoyances and bureaucracy. I'd grown up with more than enough of the latter in my life.

Risking the ire of a powerful, secretive organisation like these wizards was therefore the stupid option. Could I even realistically think about defying such a group?

You defied your father.

That thought gave me a chuckle. Perhaps I was a more rebellious soul than I wanted to admit. Not to mention the matter of Aalto's olive branch. It galled me that the man was dangling information in front of me, as if trying to bait a reaction out of me. At the same time, though—

"What did the wizard wish to tell you?"

Hasebe's voice startled me out of my thoughts. I glanced up to find him standing next to my table, arms crossed.

I spread my hands. "Let's get going. We need to get back to Knightsbridge."

"Aalto and Sturluson have departed," Hasebe said. "Is this the end of our involvement with them?"

Hasebe's question held more weight than he knew.

In that split second, I made a choice.

"We're on a timer, Hasebe," I said, rising to my feet and hurrying down the sidewalk. "Either we return to Reykjavik immediately and Aalto tries to convince Morgana to allow me to join their Order—"

Hasebe snorted, half a pace behind me. The courtesy phone booth was still smoking as we passed it.

"I know, it's quite prosaic," I said. "Sworn to secrecy and all that. But our other option involves the wizards performing some sort of forbidden magic to make us forget our memories of what happened. And I lose my magic on top of that."

"It has caused you and your friends much trouble. Why would forgetting your magic be a great loss?" Hasebe asked.

It was a question I'd asked myself many times over the last eight years. My Drowning—the death and rebirth that had bestowed me the magic and knowledge I possessed—had indeed brought a lot of hardship.

Cari, Amy, and I had tried to be heroes and had nearly died several times before failing miserably in the end. I'd fought against Cari misusing her magical powers and giving in to her darker nature many times during the years we shared a flat—a battle I'd ultimately lost. There were many reasons I could think of to give up my magic. Part of me thought it might even be a nice change of pace.

Then I thought back to three girls on a living room couch, discussing what they thought were superpowers. We'd all been so set on using our powers to help people, even though it had gone wrong in the end. I stood by that old desire to do good with my power, even after all this time.

And again, that power is something Father didn't give me and couldn't use to control me. How could I even think of giving something that precious up?

"I've been put in a position of power, though it's metaphysical rather than political or financial," I said. "It feels wasteful not to use that to do something good."

"And?"

My mouth quirked into a lopsided smile. "Alright, there is something else. If I give up now, that means those stodgy wizards are right and I am just a tool for them to use. I intend to show them they're mistaken. Damn their rules. I'm doing this my way."

Hasebe made an approving sound. "I thought so. There is too much fire in your soul. You could pass for an American."

"I'll take that as a compliment," I said, in a passable American accent. In my own voice I continued, "Hurry then. A few hours' sleep, then we need to pack. If we're going to outmanoeuvre wizards, we'll need every trick we have."

"Finally," Hasebe said. "Now they will see what it means to underestimate an ordinary man."

CHAPTER NINE

VALDISSON

KNIGHTSBRIDGE, UNITED KINGDOM

Even after seven and a half years of employing him, I don't think I'd ever seen Hasebe sleep.

When we got back to Knightsbridge I contacted my poor valet, whom we'd unintentionally abandoned in Johannesburg, and made it as far as the living room sofa before falling into a deep sleep. My bodyguard stood in the exact same position when I woke six hours later. The only change was a luggage case now sitting beside him with a maroon sheath slung atop it. It seemed he and Westaway had been making preparations for the trip to California while I'd slept.

"Pulling out the stops, are we?" I said, rubbing sleep from my eyes.

"I have been shamefully unprepared so far," he said.

He hefted the sheath and swept a blood-red wakizashi from it, examining the short sword's edge before hiding it away again.

"You'll get more use out of a sword than I ever did," I said.

During our failed teenage heroics, I'd brought along a modified fencing sabre and promptly been shot in the arm by men with guns and body armour. That summer had ended whatever love I'd had for swordplay. I hadn't picked up my sabre in years.

Knives, on the other hand...

I got up and went to the armoury box in my bedroom. The ornate wooden box had been a family heirloom and another bribe from my father for my sixteenth birthday. I'd repurposed it into a weapons safe instead.

I touched the thumbprint lock and popped the box open, withdrawing a thigh sheath of a dozen finger-length throwing knives. It felt good to have them again. We'd been running blind and under-equipped for too long.

"Hello, gorgeous," I said, strapping the knives to my thigh as I returned to the living room. "I missed you in South Africa."

Hasebe and I took the private lift up to the roof, each carrying a luggage case. Waiting for us was Westaway, his greying moustache as thick as always. He tapped the side of the sleek black ellipse that was my aircar, opening a swinging hatch door to a red velvet interior that wouldn't have been out of place in a swish limousine.

"How is appealing to a craftsman leading anywhere to finding Carissa?" Hasebe asked, stowing our luggage under the bench seats.

"I need allies. I especially need allies of the arcane variety." I locked eyes with him. "Think of it this way. If I'm able to successfully stop Juno from doing whatever the hell she plans on doing—from outside the framework of their order, mind—that turns me from an errant fugitive into a powerful potential ally. I become someone who is better off being appeased than angered. Perhaps even enough to share some of the wizards' resources or knowledge on finding one person in a world of billions."

Hasebe grunted. That particular tone meant he wasn't happy about the situation but didn't think it worth his time trying to talk me out of it.

He was right.

⋘∏⋙

SAN DIEGO, CALIFORNIA

I'd only been to California a handful of times, most of them before the age of sixteen. Los Angeles was too crowded, the Napa Valley was interesting, and the less said about San Francisco the better.

San Diego was altogether a much more charming place. It felt greener than the other places I'd seen in California, and the sight of the warm sands along the coast nearly made me want to drop everything and take a beach holiday. Had I been any less disciplined, I might have done it.

Instead, I stowed my new phone away and watched as Hasebe tapped a small coin-shaped device against the sheath of his wakizashi. The sword went limp, draping over his hand like a thin red belt. That done, Hasebe sculpted the sheath into a sash across his left shoulder.

"That never ceases to amaze me," I said, pushing the aircar's swing door open.

"It was repurposed from a medical tourniquet device that uses electromagnetism to maintain rigidity," Hasebe said, adjusting his blazer under the sash.

"MTM? Is that so?"

"Yes," Hasebe said. "I'd have thought your MediMerge training exposed you to the material before."

"That was in secondary school, a long time ago. It's still an amazing bit of technology, unlike a lot of this modern stuff."

Amusement danced in his dark eyes. "Is this why you prefer older films to new ones? Too much technology?"

"Says the one who watches spaghetti Westerns in his spare time," I said, with no actual heat in the words.

"Are you going to pull out those pistols, or whistle Dixie?"

I chuckled. "I still don't understand that euphemism, if I'm honest."

We made our way through the airhub onto the crowded streets, drawing the occasional glance as we walked past.

Makes sense. A Japanese man and a pale British heiress, both in white linen businesswear, striding down the pavement... even in America that's not a common sight.

After asking around a little, we were able to get a direction for the smith's shop. It was in a run-down shopping district, which seemed an odd place for a purported master wizard blacksmith to be working. In my haste to make it halfway across the world on time I'd not done as much research as I wanted. I was fairly certain these wizards wouldn't have an online presence, any road.

First impressions of the smith's shop were awful, no two ways about it. Stuffed between an obnoxious neon banner for a twenty-four hour gym and a boarded-up sandwich shop was what I presumed to be the smith's shop. Its blue canvas awning was torn and sun-bleached, with a faded sign reading "God's Hammer Metalworks" across the dirty glass shopfront.

As we paid our cab fare and approached, I saw the outline of a hammer's head behind the 'H' in the sign. A small holographic icon flickered in and out of life, claiming the shop to be open.

"I'm not thrilled, but this appears to be the place," I said, gesturing to the sign. "A hundred quid says that's a reference to Mjölnir."

Hasebe snorted. "We will see how good his craftsmanship truly is."

He pushed open the door, setting a little bell jingling.

The shop was laid out much as you'd expect. A horseshoe-shaped glass counter took up most of the shop's floor space, displaying knives, a section of handmade jewellery, and an array of art pieces made out of bits and bobs. The walls were lined with bigger pieces—axes, a couple of machetes, and a whole section of swords straight from Middle-Earth. Overall, the place was much cosier than I'd expected from its sorry exterior.

Even the man behind the counter wasn't what I'd expected. Instead of a burly tattooed man with a long beard, this olive-skinned man in a polo shirt and khaki shorts looked to be in his early forties. He could have come straight from Madrid.

"Good morning!" he called, the greeting tinged with a Spanish accent. "Looking for anything in particular?"

I strolled up to the counter, peering down at the selection of knives displayed there.

"Would you mind letting me see this one?" I asked, pointing at one of the knives.

"Certainly," the man said, tucking a strand of dark, wavy hair behind his ear. He reached down, unlocked the case, and came up with the knife I'd indicated. I took it, feeling the heft and balance.

The knife was a single-bladed thing with some kind of antler as its hilt. It was polished smooth, making a beautiful contrast with the wave-like patterns on the Damascus steel blade.

"It's a gorgeous piece," I said, flipping the knife over in my hand.

"Pretty knife for a pretty lady," the man said, shooting me a grin.

I smirked back at him as I returned the knife. "Do American girls find that charming?"

"It's a sales tactic. You'd be surprised how often it works," the man said, placing the knife back in its spot. He straightened, adjusting the collar of his pine green polo shirt. "Somehow I get the feeling you're here on other business. My name's Nic de la Cruz, by the way."

"Brooke Gilkeson," I replied, tilting my head in acknowledgement. "I was told you're a fine craftsman, particularly in the realm of..." I paused, searching for the right words. "Let's call them niche historical emblems."

Understanding lit his dark eyes. Nic nodded. "I see. You're the young English lady Finn Aalto told me might stop by today?"

"The same," I said.

"He also told me you lack a certain kind of focus," Nic said.

He held up a finger, striding around the counter to the door of his shop. Flicking off the holographic "OPEN" sign, he locked the door's deadbolt and turned back to us.

"There. Now we can speak more openly. So, you're the Third of this cycle?"

I kept my expression neutral, not letting Nic see how much his question had caught me off guard. It seemed Aalto wasn't just loose with his own people's secrets.

"I am," I replied, deciding to play a hunch. If Aalto was vouching for this man, then... "I was verified before the Althing in Reykjavik just yesterday."

Nic's eyebrows lifted. "You must have had quite the recommendation for someone I've never heard of."

"Snorri Sturluson vouched for me to the Althing," I said, wrinkling my nose. "Not that it's done much good."

"And unfortunately, you'll get no help from me here," Nic said, genuine regret in his expression. "Finn informed me of the... discreet nature of your potential visit. I regret to inform you that none of the things I sell here are made with my arcane arts. Talent, yes, but nothing magical."

Hasebe clenched his cybernetic fist, resting it hard on the counter-top. "Then we have been led astray yet again. Did I not tell you this was a fool's errand?"

Nic winced. "Please don't break my counter. Those are hellaciously expensive to replace."

For once, I was in complete agreement with Hasebe. It was quite cruel of Aalto to mislead me like this, but I supposed I ought to have seen it coming. Perhaps he'd even been ordered to do so by the Althing after the debacle in London. Surely he hadn't told me everything about his phone call. I'd gambled my magic and my memories on this meeting, and I'd lost. Badly.

Nic's voice interrupted my defeatist mental spiral.

"As I stated, I'm of no use to you in this shop," he said, emphasising the last three words, "but this isn't my smithy. I only keep this up for appearances. If you're looking for *Valdisson* Nicolás de la Cruz..."

He pulled a pen and notebook from the pocket of his khaki shorts and scribbled something on the paper before tearing it off and handing it to me.

"Stop by here around seven o'clock this evening. The raven might not have found a place to land, but let's see if I can't give the dove something for her trouble."

Biblical imagery? Really?

Relief and annoyance fought for place in my heart. Old habits had taught me that people constantly try and leave you in the dark, an attitude I'd projected onto Aalto. I'd often told my clients during counselling sessions not to make snap judgements about people in their lives, yet here I was doing the same thing.

No one's perfect, I suppose.

"Why can we not come at once to the smithy?" Hasebe said, striding over to where we stood.

"Because it's nearly time for lunch," Nic replied. "And I'll need to wait until I can close down the shop. I'm good, but no one can be in two places at once. Plus, I think the wait will be worth it, in more ways than one."

Damn these wizards and their cryptic comments. Did they all get some perverse enjoyment out of dangling carrots of information in front of people?

I let out a breath. "Very well. We'll see you at the smithy at seven o'clock. Does that antler knife come with a sheath, by the by?"

Nic's face broke out into a broad grin. "See, I told you it worked!"

Loathe as I am to admit, sometimes my father's views on anonymity and travelling incognito could be bang on the money. I booked a room with two beds in one of the local chain hotels under the name Annie Mai Chun, an illustrator and one of several false identities I'd made over the years. No one had ever commented on it. I suspected Hasebe to be a large part of the reason why. He gave my cover identity a certain amount of credence.

"Thoughts?" I asked, sinking down on the bed.

"We have been pulled around more than a disobedient dog," Hasebe said, standing stiff-backed as he looked out the window. "This whole affair bothers me."

"I'm not exactly chuffed by the way things have been going, either. I've taken a huge risk ignoring the wizards' secondhand demands, and so far that risk has made questionable returns."

"Are you certain this *yokai* blacksmith will be of any aid?" Hasebe said. "He knows of our rogue mission, and so far he too has only made promises."

And references to Noah's Ark... If I'm the dove, would that make Cari the raven?

"I'm hoping to negotiate something out of him," I said, sitting up on the bed. I picked up the gorgeous knife I'd bought from Nic's little shop. "If his magical craftsmanship is as fine as this, I may be able to appeal to his professional pride."

"And you think bending the ear of the blacksmith is enough to help you stop Juno?" Hasebe ran a hand down his beard. "More of a challenge than I expected."

"It's better than paying informants and hoping something floats to us across the world the way we've been doing."

Inside, though, I was beginning to question the wisdom of my actions. Was it really worth pursuing my best friend like this? Even after all that had happened?

She did try to kill you, after all.

I winced. That had been a low point for both of us, if I was honest with myself. I'd pushed her far too hard in my desperation, and she'd retaliated. It was a tactic I knew didn't work with counseling patients, yet I'd tried it anyway. No wonder she'd snapped. What a mess we'd made.

Then the memory of that first letter drifted through my head, almost fifteen years ago. I'd written a letter to a little American girl who'd been through a horrible experience at the urging of my mother. We'd become so close over the years.

She's almost the sister I never had.

That brought tears to my eyes. I wiped them away before Hasebe could notice.

Yes, I decided. I'd never given up on Cari before, no matter how tempting it had been. There was no reason to stop now. I'd move heaven and earth to fix my best friend, no matter the cost.

≪Ո≫

Six hours later, a cab dropped us off in front of a large warehouse building, corrugated steel siding making it look like every other warehouse I'd ever seen. That changed as we walked through the parking lot. In addition to some well-manicured shrubbery, two palm trees stood on either side of a mosaic-tiled fountain in front of the entrance.

"I'm not sure this place knows what it is," I said as we approached the front doors. "It's halfway between a film studio and a workshop."

The same hammer design we'd seen at the little shopfront that morning decorated the glass doors that slid open at our approach. Only this time, it was set into the glass in something that awfully resembled gold filigree. Just what was this place?

The blonde receptionist seated behind the front desk didn't do anything to clear it up. She wore a leather apron over jeans and a pink babydoll top, the name "Jerica" embossed across the top of her apron.

"Hi!" she said, somehow making the single word five syllables. "Welcome to God's Hammer Metalworks. Do you have an appointment, or are you here for a class?"

A calendar floated up on the check-in touch panel facing us, sporting the names of several different classes and instructors. I picked up the digipen, hesitated for a moment, then wrote my fake name on the check-in screen before tapping 'enter.'

"We're Nic de la Cruz's seven o'clock," I said.

Jerica's cheery demeanour changed in an instant to something more serious. "Cool. Last appointment of the day. I'll take you back, then."

She tapped a button on her computer terminal, projecting a holographic sign that let everyone know she'd be back shortly.

"First that blue-haired guy, now you," Jerica said. "What a weird Thursday."

She led us around a corner into a cavernous workshop area. Different desks and stations were set up, some with large machines I didn't recognise. Quite a few of them had cameras set up nearby, with at least one smith recording a video presentation on whatever project he was making. Several students sat watching him, attempting to follow along.

"Never thought I'd get to meet two European wizards in one day," Jerica went on. "You seem so much classier than the other one, though. Grensons, right?"

"Custom-fitted in London by a friend of mine," I replied, glancing down at the boots I was wearing. I'd almost forgotten.

"They look hella stylish," Jerica said. "Too bad I'm stuck here with Nic for another few years. I'd love to go to London sometime. It's a beautiful city with a ton of historical significance and junk. Did you know the Romans originally founded it almost two thousand years ago? Back then it was called 'Londinium.' Isn't that neat?"

"It has its charms," I said, a suspicion crossing my mind. I played another hunch. "How long have you been his apprentice?"

"A year or so," the young woman said. She stopped cold, her eyes going wide. "Did Nic tell you about me?"

"Oh, I have my ways," I chuckled, a sense of vindictive satisfaction rising in my chest. It wasn't the girl's fault, but it felt nice to get one over on the wizards for once.

"Spooky," she said, resuming our walk. Jerica led us to a door at the very back of the workshop that belonged more to a storage room than a smith's workstation.

The apprentice knocked four times in a strange rhythm. The door opened, revealing Finn Aalto in a black turtleneck, fatigue pants, and boots shiny enough to reflect the overhead lights.

He put on an expression of polite surprise I recognised too well. "Why, if it isn't Miss Gilkeson and Hasebe! Aren't you supposed to be somewhere?"

"Hello, Wizard Aalto," I said, matching his tone. "Nice to see you again."

Hasebe snorted from behind me.

"Seems you've made your decision, then," Aalto said, dropping the faux-polite tone. "No word from Morgana or the Althing yet, but your timeframe's almost half gone."

"Don't remind me," I said.

"Is Nic still back there?" Jerica asked.

"Of course I am," Nic's voice came from inside the room. The Spaniard peered over Aalto's shoulder a moment later, wavy black hair pulled back into a short tail. "Come in, come in. This is my private workshop. You could say it's where the magic happens."

I rolled my eyes as Hasebe and I followed them into the little room.

CHAPTER TEN

WHAT NIC HAD TO SAY

Nic's workshop was as crowded a room as I'd ever seen. The wall to our left housed shelves full of neatly stacked metal ingots and a collection of leather-bound books. A pegboard filled with tools and at least five different sizes of hammers hung on the far wall just above his workbench. The remainder of the room was taken up by a small couch and some folding chairs.

Nic gestured to the chair by his bench. "Please, sit."

"What the hell, you're never that gentlemanly to me!" Jerica protested as I took the offered seat.

"I'm not training her, Jerica," Nic said, a mischievous glint in his eye. "Plus, people might get the wrong impression about our working relationship if I were overly chivalrous."

"Ewww!" Jerica said, throwing out her hands as if to ward Nic off. "Never mind. I only date guys born in the same decade, thanks."

"Precisely why I do my best to treat you like anyone else," Nic said. "No sitcom romance miscommunications here. Now, apprentice, if you wouldn't mind...?"

Jerica tugged at a blond curl. "Fine, I'll get back to the desk and my stupid casebook. You gotta explain what's going on when you're done, though."

"Not likely," Nic and I said at the same time.

Aalto snickered. As the door swung shut he leaned up against the wall, gesturing to Nic. "Now, about that item we were discussing?"

He shot me a look, as if anticipating my frustration. "I know, I'm being terrible. But I think you're going to like this surprise. I told Nic my suspicion about your focus issues, and it just so happens he had a suggestion."

"I'm making good on my olive branch, to continue with the dove metaphor from earlier today," Nic said.

He gestured at a nondescript length of wood hanging from a strand of leather on his pegboard. Angular runes were carved into it, though I couldn't make them out from where I sat.

"In the old days, wizards used walking sticks or short wooden rods as focus items," Nic continued. "Some call them focus wands, others say they're rods of blasting. The small ones are good for evocation foci."

"Could you work a knife into a focus rod?" I asked.

Nic grinned. "I did consider that. It's not beyond the scope of my skill, to be sure. But for a lady like yourself, you may want something more subtle, easier to carry with you at all times."

He reached to his workbench and picked up a slender wooden box, opening the lid to reveal a tray of jewelled rings resting on neat rows of green velvet.

"Seven?" Nic asked, wiggling his fingers.

"Left index finger is a seven and a half," I replied, not quite sure what to make of the whole situation.

If Nic or Aalto had presented this any differently, I would have turned the ring down. It sends some odd signals to offer a girl a ring after knowing her for barely a day. Nor had Nic asked for any sort of payment, which I'd have understood. Instead, neither of the two wizards seemed inclined to talk out whatever deal they'd worked out on my behalf.

What sort of trick is Aalto up to now? Is he hoping to gain something from me?

The older man leaned forward, his eyes flicking to the closed door. "Don't tell Jerica I said this, but she might have a finer grasp of detail work than even I do."

"She does?" Aalto asked, a look of confusion on his face.

"Oh, she's no good at all with death magic, but her forgework... let's just say Ivaldi might have a competitor, if he was still alive." Nic snatched up one of the rings from the box. "Anyway, this is a Martello special, made of high-grade silver with a lapis lazuli stone. One of her better pieces."

It was a simple ring with a flat, dark blue gemstone set in it. As I took the ring, I made out several runes embossed subtly in the metal. Of more note was the M-shaped rune carved into the blue gemstone's smooth surface.

"Mannaz," I said, almost by reflex. The crisscross pattern in the rune's centre made it obvious to my gift of knowledge.

"We use that one quite a bit in our work as Valdissons," Nic said, obvious pride in his voice. "In enchanting and runesmithing, Mannaz represents the inner potential of a wizard. Not a magic feather, but it should help bring some of those less intuitive gifts of yours to the fore. It can't make up for proper evocation training, before you get any ideas."

"You'd have to be a full wizard for that," Aalto chimed in. "I'm sure Hasebe can attest to the importance of conditioning."

"It is a beautiful piece," Hasebe said, giving an appreciative nod. "Fine craftsmanship is rare to see anymore. You are also correct about the discipline of the body. But we are ignoring the problem Aalto-san came to discuss with you."

Nic's expression changed in an instant, much as Jerica's had earlier. "Indeed. My apologies for delaying."

"At least let me thank you for the gift before we dive in," I said, sliding the ring onto my index finger. It was a perfect fit. "It means a great deal. Thank you, Nic."

"You're welcome," Nic said, a glimmer of cheerfulness surfacing before he was all business again.

"Finn sent a telegram ahead last night to inform me of the danger." He picked up one of the books from his shelf, thumbing through it for a moment before setting it down on his workbench. "I'd heard some of the vaults were at risk, but the le Fay grimoire... if Juno gets the cipher, any number of writings in that book could be catastrophic. Based on Finn's reports of the items taken over the past several months, and my not-inconsiderable knowledge of magical ritual, I have a decent theory as to Juno's goal."

The twinkle in his eye undercut Nic's serious words, though I got the impression he was putting the former on for my benefit.

"Then you know how to stop her?" I asked. This could be my proverbial foot in the door. Nic had the upper hand thanks to his gift of the focus ring, but surely I'd be able to negotiate some sort of assistance from him.

"Of course I do," Nic said. "I'm also the only other wizard in the world who could ensure her success. Not that she knows about either of us, mind you. I tend to keep somewhat of a low profile, and Jerica doesn't exist in the magical community yet."

"The Althing was concerned Juno would try to coerce information out of him," Aalto said. "Or worse. That's why I'm here, to warn Nic in case she finds out about him."

"Juno has bigger problems," Nic said, settling onto the little couch. "If I'm correct, she's playing with forces she thinks she can control and is almost certainly wrong. Have you heard of the Nidhogg serpent?"

"My best friend has a doctorate in world mythology," I said, racking my brain. "The name sounds like something she brought up once or twice."

"Nidhogg," Aalto said, "is an honest-to-God dragon from Norse folklore—wings, fiery breath, the whole kit."

"So now Nidhogg is real, too?"

"No, it's been real this whole time," Nic said.

"What does a *yokai* dragon have to do with Juno?" Hasebe asked. "In Japan, dragons are wise and revered creatures."

"Western folklore is not as kind to the beasts, I'm afraid," Nic said, reaching past Aalto's head to the workbench. He picked up the book he'd selected earlier, flipping through weathered pages with a finger before stopping halfway down one page.

"Dragons in the west were creations of the Aesir—the first wizards—in the Viking Age," Nic said, tracing a line of text with his finger. "They were never supposed to exist. The Nidhogg serpent was the youngest and became the strongest by devouring its competition. Morgana banished it to the Wilds nine hundred years ago for fear of what havoc its immense magical power could wreak. Stories say that even Odin feared Nidhogg's power, that the dragon could be the end of the world. Ragnarök. I think Juno is trying to summon it back."

Silence descended on the room as Nic's words sank in.

Yesterday all I'd been after was my best friend. Now I'd fallen into a world where dragons and wizards were real. I'd known there was more to my world, the magic had been undeniable proof of that. But this... this was all so far beyond me I felt like a child in primary school again.

Instead I forced my mental faculties to bear on our situation.

It's an essay problem. You did hundreds of them in grad school.

"If that's the case..." I trailed off, uncertain how to phrase my question. "Would it come from the Wilds or some such? Snorri's bear in London for instance? Surely dragons don't live on Earth."

"The *fylgja* is a form of summoning magic hardly anyone knows how to do anymore," Aalto said, reclining back against the wall of books. "But you're right—beasties of that nature come from a place called the Outer Wilds."

"So what are these Outer Wilds? A magical repository of creatures, or...?"

"The spirit world," Hasebe said, gesturing to the room. "They are not here, so they must be somewhere else."

"Are you sure you're not a wizard?" Nic said, eyebrows touching his hairline. "You seem remarkably astute."

"I have seen a great deal of the world," Hasebe said, flexing the fingers of his artificial hand.

"The Outer Wilds are home to all sorts of allegedly mythical creatures and beings," Aalto said. "Most of them aren't strong enough to cross over, except the fae. But they're not allowed to anymore."

I put my face in my hands. My head was beginning to throb. "Faeries too? Is everything going to turn out to be real?"

"Not everything," Nic said. "There's a sort of ecosystem to it that we've been trying to understand for centuries. Some creatures come and go. But more importantly, the Nidhogg serpent has its hidey-hole in the Outer Wilds. That's where le Fay's ritual will drag it forth from."

"You said Nidhogg was tied to the Norse apocalypse," I said. "Is that why this ritual is so dangerous?"

"Partly, yes," Nic said.

"So let me see if I've got this straight—Juno stole a book of ancient rituals intending to summon a creature here who is powerful enough to destroy the world?"

"Worse than that," Aalto said, his northern brogue thickening. "If what Nic's already told me is accurate, even the act of trying to force this thing through the barrier between the world of spirit and the world of mankind is bad. Like triggering a magical hydrogen bomb bad. It could start a chain reaction and wreak havoc on all magic in this world."

"How could one person be this powerful? She's beginning to remind me of one of the Norse gods Cari was always going on about. The Aesir, I think."

"Wizards, not gods," Aalto said, smirking.

I treated him to a wicked eye roll. "Right, beg your pardon. I've only just learned the distinction."

"Juno is a maniac," Hasebe said. "A lunatic whose sole aim is the suffering of others for her own benefit. She is even willing to destroy the world for her own power."

"Surely not," I said, glancing from Aalto to Hasebe. "That would destroy her too, wouldn't it?"

"It would," Nic said, setting his book down again. "Which is why that's almost certainly not what she intends. If our little raven succeeds in her goal, that could be as bad if not worse. There's another outcome to the Nidhogg ritual."

"Power beyond her wildest dreams? Or does she get a pet dragon?"

"The first," Nic said. "It's an old Valdisson saying that the best of us could make chains strong enough to bind a dragon in Mithgard. The saying holds some water, if my old master was right, but I never knew how you'd get a dragon from the Wilds until last night."

Aalto's brow furrowed. "So you bind the dragon and steal its power? That's—I thought that was impossible."

"Not quite," Nic said. "You bind the dragon, kill the dragon, and take its blood into you, thus absorbing its power with its lifeblood."

Hasebe swore in Japanese. "Always about power with these people. Some things never change."

"Summon the dragon, don't die, kill the dragon, become almighty," I said, thinking aloud. "A ritual like that surely requires a lot of setup and preparation. Hence her other thefts."

"And blood," Nic said, looking as grim as I'd seen him yet. "It's an old, old ritual. Someone has to die for it to kick off. If she gets the cipher, the only thing Juno will be missing is something my master thought only I capable of creating. The chains."

None of us spoke for a few seconds. I felt sick to my stomach. Was Juno such a monster that she'd willingly sacrifice another person's life for the sake of her own power? Far worse had been done in the name of personal power, but that was hundreds of years ago.

Perhaps Hasebe was right. Some things never change.

The hairs on the back of my neck stood up at a surge of magical energy, as though something had cracked. A shriek cut through the night's stillness, followed by the sound of shattering glass.

Nic shot to his feet, grabbing the wooden focus rod from his pegboard.

"That was Jerica," he said. "If something's broken through my wards, this is going to be bad."

CHAPTER ELEVEN

FACE-OFF

A alto slid a leather driving glove over his left hand. "We have to hurry. It could be Juno."

Hasebe unfurled his wakizashi, gripping it in his cybernetic hand. He strode to the door and peeked out just as a synthetic female voice called, "De la Cruz!"

Nic's name echoed through the empty workshop. The older wizard stepped out, hands raised at his sides.

"What have you done to my apprentice?" he said.

"Don't worry, she's still alive. For now."

I poked my head around the corner. Juno was standing in the centre of the workshop, illuminated by an overhead spotlight. Her outfit was exactly the same as before, though the glossy black helmet had a blue glow to it this time. A hand poked out from the corner of the workshop nearest the reception desk. That wasn't a good sign for the girl.

Nic said, "How did you get through my wards?"

Juno rolled her shoulders in a shrug. "Wasn't hard. This place can't decide if it's a business or a fortress. I smashed in your front doors with barely any resistance."

Nic swore under his breath. "Thanks for pointing out a weak spot, anyway. What do you want?"

"I need the Open Chain," Juno said, pointing straight at Nic with a finger. "You're the only one outside of Reykjavik with even half the skill to make it."

"The only Valdisson you have access to, in other words," Nic said. "It's just a legend, you know. The last time someone tried to forge one was seven hundred years ago."

"If anyone has cracked the code, Nicolás de la Cruz, it's you," Juno said, taking a step forward. "We both know your reputation."

"One more step and I'll drown you where you stand," Aalto said, gravel in his voice as he stepped out to stand behind Nic.

"Oh, you again," Juno said, tilting her helmeted head to one side. "I thought I dropped a car on you in London."

"You missed."

"I have a shot," Hasebe murmured from beside me in Japanese. He'd ducked back around the door and was holding his Cobalt in a double-handed shooter's grip.

"Are you certain you can kill her in one shot?" I asked, matching his tone and language.

"She is still flesh and blood," Hasebe said, sighting down the revolver. "A bullet in the head is all I need to put her down."

"Where's the old man?" Juno asked while we were talking. "Or have you reached your quota of spectral bears for the week?"

Aalto barked something witty at her, standing his ground. I was too busy thinking.

It was one thing to order my bodyguard to shoot someone in cold blood. Taking a life is never an easy thing to do, despite how the cinema makes it look.

On the other hand, Juno was perfectly willing herself to sacrifice an innocent person's life. Not to mention what she might have already done to Jerica.

"Give it a twenty-count, then drop her," I said, winter's bite in my voice. "If she doesn't say anything useful, fire at ten."

"Finally," Hasebe said.

"I'm not getting any younger, de la Cruz," Juno said, synthetic voice buzzing. *"Give me the information, now. Tell me how to forge the Open Chain."*

Power stirred around her as she spoke, and Juno's last two sentences sparked with it. I'd dealt with this one before.

To a weak mind, those words would have been infused with an undeniable Suggestion to comply. Illusion magic at its finest. The problem was that if you knew how the magic worked, or your will was strong enough, it did nothing.

Nic had both.

"Nice try, *seidhkona*," he said, raising his left fist. "Now get out of my smithy before I throw you out on your—"

Hasebe's gun boomed, making me jump. Juno staggered back, dropping to one knee as Jerica stumbled and fell against a large work table on wheels. A huge crack bloomed across her helmet, but the shot hadn't killed Juno. The helmet had been sturdier than expected.

I darted out into the main workshop area, calling up my magic as I snapped my left hand out.

"Uruz!"

Invisible force surged from my outstretched hand, sending Juno, Aalto, and Nic crashing to the floor along with the table Jerica had been leaning on.

I blinked.

Perhaps Aalto had been right about this whole focus item business. That sort of death magic usually would take everything I had, and now I was barely winded.

Juno let out a bellow of rage, slamming her fist into the concrete floor. *"Kenaz!"*

Fire surged through the floor in a jagged line, bursting up into a knee-high line of flames. I dodged to the left, pumped my fist like racking a shotgun, and barked out the force rune again. As I did, I imagined twisting the knob on a radio to reduce its wavelength.

The burst of invisible force wasn't quite as wide this time, but it still caught Aalto again along with snuffing out Juno's flame wall. She rolled, kicking herself to her feet and stared at me through the broken helmet. Aalto rolled into a crouch, ducking down behind one of the still-standing workbenches.

"I've had just about enough of your meddling!" she snarled, raising a fist. *"Kenaz!"*

I knew the lance of flame was coming, but it missed me by far less than I liked.

Gunfire rang out through the workshop as Hasebe sighted on Juno again. His second and third shots missed, sparking off the floor and another work table. The fourth shot grazed Juno's torso, but before she could get off another fiery bolt, Aalto snapped, *"Laguz!"*

Juno's masked face whipped in his direction just in time to catch a dripping ball of water. It exploded like a snowball, showering water all over her.

That gave me a thought. I voiced it in a pair of syllables I hadn't heard in eight years.

"Isa!"

Juno lifted her foot as if to take a step. She was stalled by the wave of ice that spread across two thirds of her body, water freezing solid in a heartbeat wherever it touched her. I felt a flash of pride. I'd never used ice magic before. That had been Amy's bit.

That gave Nic enough time to scramble to his feet, sweeping hair back from his face as he readied his focus rod. "There are four of us, Juno. Walk away and stop this madness before you get hurt."

"There were four of you in London, too," she snarled. The inside of her helmet began to glow a bright blue, though not enough to illuminate her face. She slammed her free fist onto the ice covering her chest and spat, *"Hagalaz!"*

Every light in the workshop shorted out, dying in little puffs of smoke and sparks that plunged the warehouse into darkness. Even the light of Juno's helmet vanished, replaced by a growing cloud of fog.

"Do you know how expensive those lights are?" Nic said. "Now you're just being cruel."

There was no answer.

Hasebe strode past me, gun tracking through the fog. "I will not let her escape this time."

The clatter of footsteps on concrete rang out in the cavernous workshop. I couldn't make out where they were coming from. That is, until a woman screamed from across the workshop.

"Let me go!"

It was Jerica's voice.

"Ingwaz," Nic hissed, slashing his hand through the fog. A gust of wind mirrored his motion, cutting through the fog enough for us to see two figures across the room.

Juno, the interior of her helmet still glowing blue, had Jerica's arm twisted behind her back in a martial arts grapple lock. If the blonde girl moved she'd dislocate her shoulder, or worse.

Nic took a step towards the centre of the room, less than ten feet from where we'd clustered together in the fog. "Let go of my apprentice and we can talk, Juno."

The hushed sounds of a girl crying underscored Juno's next words.

"Nice try. We both know I'm in control here as long as I have the girl."

"Then what will it take for you to let her go?" Nic asked.

"I'm a fair woman," Juno said. "I'll accept a straight trade. You come with me, I don't break the girl."

"And if I refuse?"

Juno twisted Jerica's wrist, causing the girl to cry out in pain.

"I do more than break her."

"Bitch," I hissed. "Does life hold no value for you at all, Juno?"

"What's one life compared to saving the world?" Juno said.

Aalto let out a bitter laugh, leaning back against another piece of equipment. "How the hell can you possibly save the world? Tear it down and create a new one?"

"Quit stalling," Juno said. "What will it be, de la Cruz? Your life, or the girl's?"

Without missing a beat, Nic replied, "Mine. Let her go."

"No tricks," Juno said. "Swear that you'll come with me and give me what I want."

"What good is the word of an honest man to an oathbreaker?" Hasebe's voice rang out. "You betrayed your fellow wizards and even now try to kill one of them."

"Idiot. I was never part of the White Order, or the Keepers," Juno said, spitting out the names like they tasted off. "Those pretentious fools have egos the size of this state. The idea that someone powerful enough to challenge them exists outside their control is an absolute anathema."

So it isn't just me. I hate that I agree with Juno, but...

Juno pulled Jerica close enough that the girl was mostly in front of her, facing us. I grimaced. She'd recognised the danger Hasebe presented and was shielding herself with the blonde apprentice.

I glanced at Aalto, but his expression gave nothing away. His eyes were fixed on Nic's face.

"I swear, I'll let the girl go if you come with me," Juno said. "On the bind-rune."

She flicked up her left hand, leaving a shimmering blue image of the Jera rune in midair. Its two open angles almost touched each other, flickering as if made of candle-flame.

Nic dipped his head in a slow nod.

"I swear, on the bind-rune," Nic said, holding his hand to his heart. "I'll come. No tricks."

He held up both hands and began to approach Juno.

From behind me, Hasebe hissed a breath between his teeth. I knew this was more than he could stand. It had to be Nic's call, though. We were in his domain and Jerica was his apprentice, the fate of the world be damned.

Magic stirred in the air. Jerica's tear-streaked face had been replaced with an expression of fierce concentration, her irises blazing gold as she cried, *"Nauthiz!"*

One of the light fixtures overhead stirred, making currents in the fog. Power stirred around both the girl and the light, but it was faint and wobbly.

"No!" Nic cried, his eyes going wide in the dim light. "Jerica, don't!"

Jerica screamed, but her voice was a cry of challenge rather than pain. She threw an elbow back toward Juno, who twisted to the side.

"Are you trying to make me hurt you more?" Juno snapped. "I'd rather not. You aren't worth the trouble."

Jerica started to say something, but her words slurred together. She slumped backward against Juno's chest, her arm still tucked awkwardly behind her. Juno stumbled but kept her grip on the girl. The light fixture stopped shaking, swaying back and forth in the still room.

Nic rushed toward the pair, pausing when Juno held up a glossy pistol and aimed it at him. Blood trickled from Jerica's nose and mouth as Juno let her slump to the floor, running down her face and ruining her cute top. Nic raised his hands, kneeling down before the limp form of his apprentice. He put a finger to the side of her neck, holding it there for a few moments.

"Is she dead?" Hasebe said, glancing at Aalto.

"No. She just pushed herself too hard. Used too much of her well of power for something she knows she can't do."

Jerica began to stir as Nic stood. The older man tapped the illusory rune and nodded at Juno, who lowered her gun and waved her hand. The rune disappeared.

"Satisfied? Let's go, de la Cruz. We're burning midnight."

"No... Nic, don't do it," Jerica murmured, her voice tiny in the large room.

Nic stooped down again and whispered something to his apprentice. It was faint, but I heard the words 'Leonidas' and 'upper shelf' before Juno dragged him towards the reception desk. As they walked Nic turned to face us, a solemn expression on his face.

A car pulled up outside the workshop, headlamps shining in through the broken glass beside the front desk. The twin beams of light illuminated Juno and Nic, as though the masked woman was a valkyrie taking the wizard smith off to the afterlife.

A roar of primal fury rang out behind me. I spun just as Hasebe sighted on Juno again and fired the last three rounds in his Cobalt.

Nic ducked to one side, two of the bullets striking Juno's already damaged mask. That was enough to shatter it completely, blue light spilling out and adding a hellish ambiance to the remnants of the fog.

Juno grabbed Nic's upper arm and threw down another smoke grenade from a belt holster, both of them disappearing into the cloud of reddish smoke. Seconds later, car doors slammed and tyres squealed as the car shot off into the darkening night.

Hasebe charged past me into the cloud of smoke, Aalto not far behind.

I couldn't force my body to move. Not just because of Jerica's critical state, though that certainly didn't help. I couldn't move because of Juno.

Or rather, the glimpse I'd gotten of her face when the helmet broke.

Under her mask, Juno was a woman much the same age as myself. Her features were more gaunt and angular than the last time I'd seen them, but the scar over her left eyebrow and her flaming strands of fiery blue hair were unmistakable.

I wished I'd have been wrong. I wished it had been someone else. But I knew that face too well. I'd seen it almost daily for over half my life.

It was her.

Carissa Edwards, my best friend, was Juno.

CHAPTER TWELVE

OLD, UNHAPPY, FAR-OFF THINGS

B reak room coffee is terrible, but I was grateful Jerica had recovered enough to make me some anyway. Though unsteady on her feet, the girl was made of sterner stuff than she appeared at first glance.

An emergency generator had started up after the escape, providing a few scattered lights across the various spaces. We hadn't called the police, and they didn't seem to have noticed all the commotion yet. It was a small mercy I gladly accepted.

The young apprentice was the only one to have spoken since Hasebe and Aalto returned. Both men were covered in red dust from the smoke grenade.

Jerica handed each of them a coffee as well, her whole front still covered in blood from her nose. "Here. I know it's late, but coffee cheers me up when... when things aren't going well."

Hasebe accepted a cup. Aalto held up a hand in refusal, sitting down at one of the tables. I stood and walked out of the break room, back into the workshop.

I still couldn't speak. My bodyguard had been right about far more of this than I was comfortable with. Including his speculation about Juno's identity.

Cari... how could you?

I hadn't wanted to believe it. The truth was, it made too much sense. She'd gone a bit off the deep end during our last year of grad school together, stewing in her own regrets and bitterness until they poisoned her heart.

I still didn't want to believe she'd be willing to murder someone for power. The killing of her ex-boyfriend, while terribly immoral, had at least had some justification based on the trauma and abuse she'd experienced at his hands. It wasn't right, but I could understand it.

Not this.

Stealing magical artefacts, kidnapping, planning to murder some innocent person in a magic ritual... What had my best friend become? Did anything remain of the ambitious little girl who'd bought me *The Iliad* for my fourteenth birthday?

More and more memories flooded back. I couldn't stem the flow, silent tears running down my cheeks as I stared out at the dim workshop. The heavy use of my magic had left me exhausted, even with the focus ring aiding my efforts. I'd need a good long sleep to recover.

"If I didn't know better I'd think you've seen a ghost," Aalto said, leaning against the wall beside me.

When I didn't reply he added, "It was Nic's decision. May have been a bad one, but if he's right about Jerica's skills maybe this is the lesser of two bad outcomes."

"She's here," I said, my voice a whisper.

"Hm?"

"She's here," I repeated, forcing air across my vocal cords. My voice still came out quivering and tiny.

"You saw her face?"

I tilted my head.

"You... recognized her face?"

I nodded again.

"Brooke, this is critical," Aalto said, grasping my arm. "Even Snorri doesn't have that intel. If we know who Juno is, we might be able to predict where she's going next. We might still have a chance of stopping her before she gets the cipher. Who is she?"

Do I even know anymore?

Aalto's face was streaked with shadows from the odd lighting and grimy with smoke dust. He reminded me of an old barbarian warrior I'd seen once on TV, face painted to strike fear in the hearts of his enemies. The effect on me wasn't much different.

If I revealed what I knew, would Aalto try to kill Cari? Would his opinion of me be altered, knowing that I was once friends with a power-crazed rogue witch?

Do I care what he thinks of me?

I snuffled, wiping my cheeks with the back of my hand. "I can tell you a little. But you have to promise me something first."

"Now is not a time to be bargaining, Brooke."

"Then you'll get nothing from me," I snapped, my composure and patience gone. "I've had it with you people treating me as I'm some tool for your benefit. Holding out on me for not belonging to your bloody society, being suspicious of me even though I've done nothing to you..."

"That's not what—"

"Don't act like you're not part of this, Aalto. You've been just as pompous and cryptic as the others, only they never pretended they'd explain anything first."

I began pacing, unable to stay still any longer. "Why did you go out of your way to get me here? Were you hoping I'd come after you just to get killed in the crossfire? Solve your interloper problem before it became a problem?"

"Because I respect you."

I spun to face him. Aalto stood there, hands in his fatigue pockets. In the dim light he looked chagrined, rather than angry.

"I know it may be hard to believe," he said, "but I invited you here because I think you've got a lot of potential."

"You and Snorri keep saying that, but that doesn't change the fact that you've both kept me out of the loop the entire time Hasebe and I have been with you."

"If I can make a defence," Aalto said, raising his hands, "events have been moving somewhat quickly since we met. Two days ago I didn't know you actually existed."

"Two days ago I didn't know my best friend from girlhood was trying to destroy the world," I said.

I froze, eyes locking with Aalto's as my mind caught up to my mouth. I thought a rude word.

"So that's it," he said. "Juno is someone you hold very dear."

"Well... If you must know, I've been fussing after her for most of my life. She's been through a great deal. Not that it justifies what she's doing, but..." I trailed off. What else could I say after that?

Aalto put his left hand to his heart, just as Nic had done earlier. "I swear, on the bind-rune, whatever you tell me will stay between us. Fate of the world be damned."

I took a deep, shuddering breath, forcing down my raging emotions. Duct tape would have to hold my broken heart together for now. "If I'm the Third of this cycle, that would make Juno... Cari, one of the first two. I don't know which one of them actually went in first."

Aalto sucked in a breath. "Holy hell... that explains a few things."

"We were barely eighteen," I said. "We almost died in a hoverboat crash and thought we'd be marooned on that little island. There was some sort of scuffle and Cari fell in the pool. The Lock. Whatever you called it. It wasn't quite a proper Drowning, but..."

"That doesn't seem to matter all that much for the Nine. No wonder her magic is so strong. She didn't even look all that winded by any of it."

"The point is, I've known Cari since we were nine years old. She is a traumatised and unwell woman, and I've been looking for her ever since she murdered her ex-boyfriend and disappeared."

Aalto's expression fell. "She killed him with magic?"

"I can't imagine it was anything else. Unfortunately. She wasn't always the most discerning with her power, and he was horrible to her."

"That complicates things," he said. "If she's killed with magic... well, it's like any other form of murder. It stains the soul."

"Can she be brought back?"

"I doubt it. You can't do magic you don't believe in, let alone what the Codex adds about the wielding of lethal magicks against another of mankind."

"She's a good person," I said, making a fist. "I know she is. It's still in there somewhere."

Aalto exhaled through his nose. "Your friend has to want to be saved in order for there to be any kind of atonement or restoration. She seemed a little angry."

"She is," I said. "She's always been a little hot-tempered, but this... I still can't believe it."

"Your reaction says otherwise."

"That's beside the point. I've been after Cari for two years and this is the first time I've seen her in the flesh."

"So in other words," Aalto said, "you have no idea where she is or where she'd be taking Nic."

"That's about the size of it," I said. "Perhaps I am just making this whole mess worse after all."

"No you aren't."

The speed and forcefulness of his rebuttal caught me off guard. I was about to ask what he meant when Jerica squealed from inside the break room. It seemed to be a sound she made quite often.

"The book!" she said, stumbling past us. "Omigod, the book!"

Hasebe emerged from the break room, staring after Jerica.

"Excitable, that one," he commented.

"What did you say, Hasebe?" I asked, watching as Jerica sprinted through the workshop like a baby giraffe.

"Did you not hear Nicolás comment on Leonidas?" Hasebe said. "For a man who thinks he may be about to die, ancient history seems an odd place for the mind to turn."

"Guys!" Jerica called, standing in front of the door to Nic's private workshop. "I think I know how to find where he's taking Juno!"

⫷∏⫸

Several minutes later, the three of us were peering over Jerica's shoulder as she leafed through pages of a book she'd pulled off Nic's topmost shelf.

"Explain this whole coded message thing again," Aalto said. "I still don't understand how you got 'find my notes in a book from my workshop' from 'hey, that ancient Spartan king was pretty neat.'"

"So, like," Jerica began. "You're with the Order, you know how much random junk you have to memorise as an apprentice. Nic knows I love ancient history and turned it into a teaching game or whatever. He brings random junk like that up all the time just to see if I'm paying attention."

I exchanged a look with Hasebe. The girl had some depth, more than either of us had thought.

Alto massaged his chin, now covered in a day's worth of stubble. "So he'd say, 'the sacking of Jerusalem by Rome was bad,' or something, and you'd go get a blue book and look for page seventy?"

"You got it!" Jerica said.

"Good thing he only has a couple dozen books in here," Aalto said under his breath.

"No wonder wizards are so damn cryptic," I said, "if this is a normal method of instruction for them. So 'Leonidas' and 'upper shelf' told you—"

"Top shelf, red book for Sparta, page 480 since that's the year the Battle of Thermopylae took place." Jerica giggled. "Here it is! I still got it."

Am I really only half a dozen years older than her?

She turned one last page, revealing two whole pages filled with drawings and diagrams. Notes in a rough, spidery hand filled in most of the gaps. It looked a mess.

Across the top of the first page was written, "Gleipnir, the Open Chain: Speculations on its Construction and Forging." Six bullet points were written below, accompanied by a copious amount of notes around each one.

I read the six points aloud. "The noise of a cat's footfall, a woman's beard, the root of a mountain, a bear's sinew, a fish's breath, and a bird's spittle."

"Weird," Jerica said. "Like, all of that sounds super fake."

"The thought seems to be that none of those items are real, so it's useless to struggle against them," Aalto said, reading from a different part of the page. "Makes sense if you're trying to keep a giant wolf from eating your face off, as the story goes."

"So how does one forge something out of items that don't exist?" I said.

Jerica tapped against the page with a painted nail. "Nic told me his old master spent almost a hundred and seventy years trying to figure out the material components of some smithing project. I think this is it."

I glanced down at the line she was pointing to. Sure enough, the spidery handwriting had tried to puzzle out items that could be logically assumed to be those components.

'Cat's footfall = John Cage?' one note read. *'4:33 track is literally the sounds of silence. Investigate Simon & Garfunkel??'*

Similar statements and ideas filled the margins, but some of the writing was clearer, in a neater and more legible ink. It matched the handwritten receipt for my new antler-handle knife.

"Jerica," Aalto asked. "Where would Nic go to collect any of these items written here?"

I snorted. "Surely he can't find any of it wholesale. Tesco's selection isn't that wide."

"I keep telling him about the cool runecanting stuff I could get up to with nail polish," Jerica said. "But if Nic's really being forced to make this crazy project for some crazy wizard chick, there are a few people he'd talk to."

She went back to Nic's bookshelf and selected another volume. This one was only the size of her hand, bound in dark leather.

"Nic knows people all over the world who get him random junk for wizard projects. If he's not working here, he'd have to order or requisition some really specialised stuff."

Hasebe nodded. "I know several gunsmiths who have made their own personalised tools, since their needs are so specific."

"Exactly!" Jerica said, opening the smaller book. All down one page was a list of names, followed by a city, phone numbers, and an item listed after each. The items ranged from obsidian chips to arctic wolf teeth to denatured spider's venom.

I didn't know it was possible to denature spider's venom.

"Nic's list of suppliers?" I guessed.

"Looks that way," Aalto said. "We'll never get anywhere checking these one by one, though. There must be forty or fifty names here."

"Look for any that specify smithing tools or metalworking," Hasebe instructed. "If he is making a chain, that will narrow our list."

"According to myth, Gleipnir was a silken cord used to bind the dreaded wolf Fenrir, since no other chains would hold him due to his insurmountable strength," Jerica said, peering at Nic's research notes. "I dunno, though... you could probably still use woven metal to make a cord like that. Would take some seriously precise technique, but worth a shot."

Sure enough, our list shrank to five names. Two were in Mexico, one in Prague, and one in Norway. The third name on the list, Cal Onasis, was from Athens.

I glanced at Aalto to find him giving me a look of incredulity.

"It can't be that simple... can it?"

"You tell me, oh master of obfuscation," I shot back. "Are we going to Greece based on a hunch and an old book?"

"I mean, it's not like you have any other leads," Jerica said. Her face fell. "And, uh... I kinda don't want my *sensei* to die, either."

"Might be our best shot," Aalto said. "We've got to stop Juno either way. Now we know what she's up to and where she might be."

"Ooh, can you call in the Keepers?" Jerica asked. The apprentice wizard shot up and started reaching for her phone. "Nic gave me the secure landline number, we can call and get them—"

"Let's not be hasty," I interrupted. In all the excitement, I'd nearly forgotten about the secondhand threat from the Keepers. "We have other allies to call in first."

"Other allies?" Jerica said, sounding incredulous. "Who the hell do you know that's better than the Keepers? This is my *sensei* we're talking about! We need everybody we can get."

"Aalto, can you get a message to Snorri?" I asked, turning to him. "He's the right kind of firepower we could use, and somewhat more discreet."

"Probably," he replied, leaning back against Nic's bookshelf. "He should be back from Oslo by now."

"Okay seriously," Jerica said, folding her arms over her chest. "What's your problem with the Keepers? That's the obvious solution, and I can't help but think you're dodging them. Do you not care about Nic?"

"Jerica, I have no wish for Nic to come to any harm," I said, trying to speak gently. "I also don't want to turn this into a full-blown manhunt. Ca—*Juno* is more apt to kill Nic if she thinks we've sent the bloody Royal Marines after her."

I could barely get the name out. It still hurt my heart too much. But I also got the sense that Jerica wouldn't let the matter drop. I'd have to clue her in to get her to leave it.

Hasebe clenched his cybernetic fist.

"And if you must know," I said, letting out a heavy sigh, "by now the Keepers are trying to find and re-educate Hasebe and I. Nic seems outside their hierarchy and influence, so I came to ask him for help. We'd appreciate them not knowing exactly where we are at the moment, thanks."

Jerica had been on the verge of an angry comment. That stopped her, eyes going wide. "You... what? Holy crap—what did you do?"

Before I could answer, Jerica's eyes flared in anger again. The golden fire in her eyes translated to a literal orb of fire around her left hand.

Hasebe's wakizashi was in his hand before I saw him move, one quick thrust away from the girl's ribs.

"So it's all your fault! You're gonna get Nic killed!" She turned on Aalto. "Can't you, like, arrest her or something? She's obstructing an investigation, and—"

"Stand down, Wizard Martello," Aalto said, his intonation eerily similar to Morgana's when she'd used her official voice. "I'm aware of the situation, and I'm handling it."

"But—"

"Shall I repeat myself?" Aalto said, standing to his full height. "We'll get him back, Jerica. Mark my words. But we've got to be smart about it. Brooke's safety is my concern, too."

Jerica and I shot each other a confused glance before turning the expression to Aalto. His face was set in stone, a very Hasebe-esque expression.

"For your own sake, girl," Hasebe himself interjected, "don't do anything foolish. I will gut you like a fish."

Jerica's gaze flicked to Hasebe, as if she'd only just remembered he was there. Then her lip quivered.

"Okay," she stammered. The fire in her hand died away as she burst into tears, burying her face in her hands.

"I'm sorry!" she wailed. "I'm just so scared. Nothing like this has ever happened before! And I almost killed myself with my own freakin' magic! I'm no good at anything but enchanting."

It was then that I realised just how old I felt. Minding Cari for so long and discovering my dad's true nature as a teenager had aged me much more than I'd ever thought.

"Hush now, don't cry," I said, in the motherly voice I hadn't used for so long. "We'll take care of Nic. I promise. I'm too far in to stop now."

You're going to run out of luck sooner or later, a little voice in my head whispered. *The messier this gets, the more probable it all crashes down on you.*

"And brings me closer to Cari," I said under my breath. "She has a lot more to answer for now. I have to make her explain. I have to understand."

CHAPTER THIRTEEN

RECONNAISSANCE

ATHENS, GREECE

B etween Hasebe and Aalto, Jerica had been convinced to stay behind in San Diego. Hasebe's main argument was that her training wasn't far enough along for her to be anything but a liability, which Aalto echoed.

"Besides," he'd added, "Someone has to try and cover for Nic. It'll be much less suspicious if people just think he's gone off on another supply run."

The logic completely failed to explain why Aalto continued to involve me in this whole mess, but I wasn't about to bow out now in any case. It had become too personal.

Jerica hadn't liked it, but she came 'round and agreed. She then set about getting an emergency glass-cutter to come in and replace the smithy's shattered front doors.

I was starting to be impressed with the blonde apprentice. Despite the maddeningly cryptic wizard behaviour Nic had exhibited, he was more cultured and intelligent than he suggested. Jerica exhibited much the same qualities, which I suspected was why he'd chosen her as his apprentice in the first place.

With all that sorted, and one transatlantic aircar flight later, we touched down in Athens.

Athens was far warmer than Johannesburg had been. Even my lighter wardrobe for our visit to California felt stifling in the sunlight. Finn had swapped his black leather jacket for an outer layer resembling a kimono. It was offset by his dark blue hair, making for an interesting contrast.

If that doesn't sum him up in a nutshell.

Snorri was waiting for us at a cafe just on the edge of the Monastiraki market district in Athens. The big man looked dour, only a hint of his easygoing nature peeking through as we approached. Today he was dressed in another expensive suit, this one a pastel blue colour.

"Oslo was raided two hours before I arrived," Snorri said by way of greeting, finishing off a cup of something in one swallow. "She made off with the cipher book."

His mood abruptly made more sense

Aalto swore in Gaelic. "That's it, then. Juno almost has everything she needs. We need to move."

We caught Snorri up to speed on the events in San Diego, as well as Nic's prediction of Juno's goal.

"Nicolás is a good man, and a damn fine rune-canter," Snorri said, slowing his pace to keep up with us. "I don't want to think about what that girl might do to him."

"He is too valuable to harm," Hasebe countered. "Not until he has accomplished Juno's goal."

"He's going to need a great deal of equipment and tools for whatever undertaking Juno has in mind." Snorri stroked his long beard. "Perhaps even working in her own smithy."

"Are those hard to come by?" I asked.

Snorri shrugged, bumping the top of his head against a floating sign as we passed under it. "There are only half a dozen Sons of Ivaldi left in the world. Many of the great masters have passed on. It takes a great deal of time for a smith to learn exactly what kinds of tools he needs."

"One of the notes in Nic's book equated the 'root of a mountain' to a precious metal mined out of the earth," Aalto said, adjusting his sunglasses. "We suspect that regardless of tools, Juno is going to need a lot of raw materials for these chains. Onasis is as good a starting point as any."

"Callum Onasis?" Snorri asked. "The silversmith?"

"Of course you know him," I said, rolling my eyes.

"I've never met the man, but I'm quite familiar with his work. He created a protective circle for me a few dozen years ago for use in my workshop. Finest work I've seen in a long time."

"Hopefully he tells us something," Hasebe said. "Juno has a large head start."

That dour observation seemed to kill off any other attempt at conversation. We picked up our pace and made our way through the bustling city. Ultramodern holodisplays showed prices of small stalls smushed between ancient stone shops that had been in use for over a thousand years. A drone hovered by, displaying an advert for a tour of the Parthenon.

The more things change, I suppose...

One of the drone's rotors sputtered and died as we passed, sending it spinning to the ground. Hasebe chuckled.

This time of year, and this close to the centre of Athens, there were people everywhere. I chewed on my lip, keeping behind Hasebe as he cleared me a path through the crowd. His movements were rougher than usual, but then again, we did stand out quite a lot.

Damn suit is far too conspicuous, even here. This would be an awful place for the Keepers to find us.

Onasis' shop didn't stand out much from other shops we'd passed, though I got the sense that it was a fair bit smaller. It looked to be one of the older buildings in the market, meaning there weren't any windows facing us on this side.

We pushed past a heavy glass door into a well-lit room. To our right was a glass case filled with rows and rows of rings and necklaces, some of the proprietor's handiwork. Larger pieces hung from strings and were displayed on the walls.

In front of an archway across from the entrance sat a solid wooden table, a well-dressed man and a boy seated in chairs around it. The man smiled at us as we entered, his thick moustache bristling. He stood, spreading his arms wide.

"Good afternoon and welcome! I am Callum Onasis, owner of this shop. What can I interest you fine people in today?"

"Information, if you don't mind," I said. I didn't have time to play the diplomat. "We're looking for a fellow smith who may have come by for some supplies. It's imperative that we learn what's become of him."

The man's smile remained, but his dark eyes hardened. "I see, I see. I want no trouble in my shop, madam and sirs."

Aalto gathered power and whispered a word, flicking two fingers up in a short vertical slash followed by an X between the lines he'd made. The M-shaped Mannaz rune shimmered to life, a translucent illusion matching the rune in my focus ring.

"Business from the High Althing," Finn said, the rune hanging in the air before him. "It's alright."

Onasis' expression froze on his face. Then he cleared his throat, his shoulders relaxing.

"Your pardon, miss. It seems I misjudged you."

He turned to the boy, speaking in a burst of what I assumed to be Greek. The boy scampered off to the back of the shop, disappearing around the corner of the archway.

"As it happens," Onasis continued in English, "I saw an old friend yesterday whom I haven't spoken to in years. Strolled into my shop like he'd been here just last week instead of last century."

"That would be Nicolás de la Cruz, then?" I said.

"It would indeed." Onasis leaned against the glass jewellery case, resting on his broad forearms. "Is Nicolás in some sort of trouble?"

I exchanged a glance with Aalto before saying, "The short answer is yes."

"Anything I can do to help, tell me. He's one of my best customers."

"Did he purchase any specialised tools or materials from you?" Hasebe asked.

"He did, as a matter of fact." Onasis hurried around the archway and returned carrying a monstrous leather-bound book with the month and year embossed on it. Snorri, whom I hadn't noticed lagging behind, wedged his way into the small shop. He had to turn sideways to fit his broad shoulders through the entryway.

Onasis set his large book down on the wooden table with a thump, flipping pages until coming to a stop at the previous day's date. "Nicolás bought... two heavy smithing hammers, a set of angled tongs reinforced by magic, and thirty troy ounces of silver in ingots."

Snorri whistled. "A lord's ransom, in the old days."

"Was he with anyone?" I asked. "A young woman wearing a mask, perhaps?"

"There was a young woman that came in a few minutes after him, I seem to remember." Onasis wrinkled his nose, making his moustache bristle again. "I didn't think they were together, though."

"What did she look like?" I pressed.

"Erm..." Onasis rubbed his chin. "Probably younger than thirty. Dark brown hair, looked vaguely military. Seemed tense. Had a notable scar over one eyebrow."

"That sounds like her," Snorri said. "Bold of the lass to show her face."

"Athens doesn't strike me as the kind of place where strolling around with a full face helmet would be overly normal," I said. "London, perhaps. Lots of people have motorcycles. San Diego... well, it's California."

Hasebe scoffed.

"Did Nic tell you anything about where he was going or what he was up to?" Aalto asked, leaning on the counter.

"He didn't," Onasis said. His expression fell. "I'm sorry."

"You've done what you could, friend." Snorri said, giving the man a reassuring smile. "It's more than we could have hoped to find here."

"Wait," Hasebe said, holding up a hand. "Do you not require your customers to sign a bill of sale for their purchases? Particularly with expensive transactions?"

We all turned to stare at him, my cheeks going pink. That was something I should have considered. Where was my brain today?

Jumping off the cliff alongside my heart, that's where.

I ground my back teeth. Cari's reappearance was hitting me far harder than I'd thought it would, given the circumstances. I hadn't wanted to think she could fall further than I'd already seen her slip.

Onasis slapped a palm to his forehead. "Why of course! How could I forget?"

He dashed into the back room again, returning a few moments later with a large three-ring binder.

"Nicolás purchased over five hundred euro-yen worth of materials from me, which means I had to get a signature from him for book-keeping reasons."

Onasis opened the binder and began turning pages, tearing one in his haste. "I knew who he was, so I didn't give the book a second glance after he'd signed it."

The olive-skinned man spun the binder to face us. He placed his hand and forearm over the page, spreading his fingers to cover all but one name. Aalto and I leaned over the table to read it.

On the page, written next to yesterday's date in Nic's neat hand-writing, was the name "S. Westin Northwaitte."

Aalto snickered. "Nic is giving dad jokes a run for their money."

My pulse quickened as the implications of the name hit me. Aalto was right, but more importantly we had another lead.

I made eye contact with Onasis and tipped my head in a nod. "Thank you, Mister Onasis. You've been immensely helpful."

The Greek man chuckled. "Just make sure Nic gets out of whatever trouble he's gotten into. He's my best customer. I'd hate to lose his business."

"We will do what we can," Hasebe said, turning away. "*Arigato gozaimashita.*"

"Thank you," I repeated in English, just in case Onasis hadn't caught it.

Snorri looked confused, glancing from me to Aalto as we exited the smith's shop and began walking down a narrow side street.

"You know what that means, don't you?" Aalto asked.

"What did you see?" Snorri asked. "I was too occupied with not blundering into any of the pieces on display."

I smirked, mostly due to the mischievous satisfaction of keeping the ever-cryptic Snorri in the dark once more. The situation was still dire, but now we had a lead.

"We need to hurry back to the airhub," I said, pulling my phone from my back pocket. It was still working, a stroke of luck after these past few days.

"Where are we going?" Snorri asked, narrowly avoiding a lamppost as he hurried to keep pace with us.

I tapped a speed dial number into my phone. It hesitated a few seconds before connecting my call.

"Westaway?" I said when my valet answered. "Be a good man and prep the aircar. We're off to Norway." I didn't wait for him to reply, tapping the button to end the call as I replaced the phone in its pocket.

"Norway?" Snorri repeated. "Did Nicolás write that in the smith's book? Surely Juno wouldn't have let him be that brazen."

"No," Aalto said. "What he actually wrote was the name 'S. Westin Northwaitte,' which if you say quickly sounds a lot like—"

"—'Western Norway,'" Snorri finished. "It's a lovely place this time of year. And the 'S'... You think the Valdisson is implying he is being held somewhere on the southwestern coast of Norway?"

"We will not know until we get there," Hasebe said. "Norway is not a small country, even with some direction."

Snorri let out a barking laugh as we turned another corner. "We've got her on the run now! If Juno's forge is in Norway, a swift strike from the Keepers can finally put an end to her."

I winced. "Snorri, have you forgotten about our little misadventure in London already? We can't bring in the Keepers. It's my head and my magic if we do."

Snorri grunted. "Of course, my apologies. Finn told me of your ultimatum. If the Althing is too short-sighted to allow you a second chance, I've got some other resources we might be able to—"

Invisible force slammed into me, sending me stumbling into a wall. My shoulder bounced off it, nearly followed by my head a second later.

Aalto bit out a word, snapping his left hand up. A quarter-dome of water flowed to life in front of him just in time to bend as it caught another burst of invisible force.

A figure in a dark green cloak jumped off the low roof of a building in front of me, throwing a punch. I was too winded to react, which meant Hasebe jumped in front of me and sliced with his wakizashi.

The figure screamed as his gloved hand tumbled through the air. I recovered enough to lash out with one foot and strike his knee.

"Run!" Aalto barked. I glanced up just in time to see a flash of dark blue as he ran past, trailed by five identical grey-and-green clad figures. Hasebe slammed his hands on either side of my attacker's head, stunning him long enough for me to pull myself to my feet.

"After him!" I said, charging past Hasebe.

We'd run out of time.

The Keepers had found us.

CHAPTER FOURTEEN

LIVE-FIRE
EXERCISING

Action films always make running from an attacker look easy. It doesn't matter how crowded the streets are, somehow the hero manages to tip over a cart of fruit or a merchant's stall and run away. Oftentimes there's a motorcycle involved, too, just for the added flair and drama.

I would have killed for a motorcycle.

My legs ached and my lungs were on fire. Hasebe grunted from behind me. I heard a rope snapping, along with a muffled grunt and a wet splat.

"Clothesline?" I called back, glancing over my shoulder. Sure enough, he'd slashed a nearby clothesline and dropped someone's drying laundry on one of the Keepers chasing us. The one now missing a hand hadn't followed us, which worried me more.

"It will keep them off of you a fraction longer," Hasebe said. He didn't even look winded. I decided I wasn't in as good of shape as I'd thought.

Up ahead, one of the five Keepers chasing Aalto hurled a loose paving stone at him. Aalto dodged, running on a wall parallel to the street for a few feet before ducking right down another side alley. I hadn't a clue where we were anymore. We'd left Adrianou Street and Onasis' shop far behind.

Something caught at my foot. Hasebe shoved me to my left as a wet jumper splattered on the cobbled street.

"Thanks," I managed, gasping for breath.

"Run. Thank me later."

None of our attackers seemed to have guns, a small mercy. We took the same right turn Aalto had made and stumbled into a small courtyard just in time for one of the Keepers to collapse to the ground in front of me.

Three of the others were trying to take Aalto to the ground. One had his arms wrapped around Aalto's chest, another was pushing him backwards, and a third was trying to wrap arms around his legs.

"*Laguz!*" I snapped, throwing out my left hand. A finger-width stream of water lashed out from my palm and slapped the Keeper gripping Aalto's legs, cracking like a bullwhip. I hadn't known I could do that. I was already tired. The power of my working made it worse.

Hasebe shoved me to the side, wedging my back into a doorway.

"Stay," he barked, then flipped his wakizashi in his hand and flung it at the Keeper trying to push Aalto down. The short sword lodged in the man's back. He screamed, jerking upright. Aalto lashed up with his knee and caught him square in the chin, sending him reeling. Hasebe charged up, grabbed his sword, and slit the man's throat.

Oh dear. That's not going to endear us to the wizards.

That thought was all I had time for as the Keeper with the missing hand charged into the courtyard, carrying a hatstand in his remaining hand. He swung at me, missing only because he'd aimed too high.

"*Uruz!*" I twisted my wrist with the word. A stone broke free from the pavement below, twisted 'round the hatstand's reach, and caught the Keeper full in his left temple. He crumpled to the ground, hatstand clattering off the stones.

Hasebe and Aalto were trading blows with the other three Keepers and seemed to be holding up alright. That is, until two more raced into the courtyard and joined in.

"How many of these stupid gits are there?" I said aloud.

"Nine!" Aalto called, ducking under a punch. "They always come in squads of nine."

"Fantastic," I said. Those odds left no room for playing nice. I kicked out at the Keeper curled on the ground, aiming for his hooded forehead. My boot connected with a sickening crack of bone. The man went limp.

I didn't give myself time to think about what I'd just done. Instead, I stood to my full height, drew up whatever power I had left, and stamped down on the stones with a cry of, *"Uruz!"*

The stones rippled out from my left foot in a wave that caught everyone in the courtyard. Aalto rolled back onto a short stairway, avoiding the attack. Hasebe, wrestling with one of the Keepers, used the opportunity to flip the man over and land atop him. The other Keepers stumbled, falling backwards atop the mess I'd made of the courtyard's stones. That would be the last of my magic, though. If I pushed it harder I might injure myself.

I might've done that already.

I yanked open my blazer, ignoring the button that went flying as I reached to my shoulder sheath and withdrew two knives. As another of the Keepers reached for Aalto again, I flicked my wrist. One knife missed, but the other embedded itself in the man's gloved hand. He reared back, exposing his neck. Aalto threw an elbow into his throat, dropping another Keeper. A quick count put us at three against six. Better odds, but not much.

Hasebe let out a war cry as he reeled back, bleeding from a gash just below his eye. He reached to his shoulder holster, drew his Cobalt, and clubbed the Keeper who'd just hit him in the stomach. When the man doubled over, Hasebe shot him twice through the crown of his head. Fluid splattered over the brawlers, too dark to be blood. Four down.

"Don't get blood on my kimono!" Aalto snapped, elbowing another Keeper in the face. "I'm out of spare clothes and blood is hard to hide."

"You're welcome," Hasebe said, but he did stow his Cobalt back in its holster.

Out of knives, I reached for my magic again and was instead hit with a wave of exhaustion which swept over me all at once. My muscles and joints ached like I'd run a marathon in stiletto boots. Blood began to dribble down over my lips.

"Hasebe, I'm going to..." I started, before blacking out.

≪Ո≫

A gentle humming brought me back to consciousness. I opened my eyes on the cabin ceiling of my aircar.

"Remember when you told me installing a home gym was 'a waste of resources?'" Hasebe's voice said from my left.

I swivelled my head. He and Aalto were seated next to each other on the wine-red leather bench seat opposite me.

"Alright then," I said, pulling myself up to a seated position. "You and Westaway can haul the treadmill up the stairs."

"Anything burnt out? Magically speaking, I mean?" Aalto asked, leaning forward. He'd stripped out of his kimono, leaving him in just a black t-shirt and his fatigue trousers. He resembled a backup dancer at a pop concert.

I took stock of my magic. It was hard to tell beyond vague impressions, but all my muscles ached and my head throbbed. Those tended to be signs that I'd overtaxed myself.

It also distracted me from thinking about the several murders we'd just committed.

"No," I said, flexing the fingers of my left hand. "But we probably shouldn't get in any more fights with the Keepers."

"Something was wrong with them," Aalto said. "They were too mechanical, too lifeless. Notice how they didn't say anything?"

That was a damn good point. They were wizards, after all. Any opportunity for these people to be cryptic and spooky was not one to be wasted. Nor had they given any kind of reading of rights, if their function as a law-enforcing group meant anything. Even the wizards in Johannesburg had spoken a few words here and there. Aalto was right.

"Come to that," I said, stretching stiff arms out to either side. "Where's Snorri?"

"Not a clue," Aalto said. "He wasn't with us when Westaway showed up."

"He vanished during our scuffle," Hasebe said, clenching his mechanical fingers so hard they creaked. "How convenient."

An odd feeling slithered through my stomach. "Aalto... how long have you and the big man been partners?"

The blue-haired wizard shrugged. "About two years. I met him a little ways into my apprenticeship with Lía, but that was four years ago."

"Has he always been this flighty?"

"Yes, actually. The man is powerful and knows a great deal, but he sort of comes and goes as he pleases. He's always struck me as something of a lone wolf, not one that gets along much with other people unless he chooses to. Though I've never seen or heard of him running from a fight."

"They may have neutralised him first," I said. This whole situation was spinning out of control.

Aalto wrinkled his nose. "I'd like to say that's not possible, but... he has been clumsier than usual lately. Maybe his age is finally getting to him."

"How many Keepers did we kill?"

"Not Keepers," Aalto corrected. "I don't know who or what they were, but they weren't Keepers. Hasebe and I each got four."

"I took out one. That's all of them, then."

A long beat passed before I added, "You're absolutely positive you didn't just murder nine of your own people?"

"Yes," Aalto said, clenching a fist. "We have more important priorities right now, anyway. Juno has to be stopped, and Nic has to be saved if we can manage that too."

"Well... alright, if you're sure."

His response carried conviction. I didn't want to press him on it. I was still a bit knackered, even if my conscience prickled with the remaining uncertainty.

"I'm positive they weren't Keepers," Aalto said. "Humanoids, maybe. I think they may have been simulacra of some kind."

"It was a good trap," Hasebe said, his English rougher and more gravelly than usual. "Whatever those *yokai* were, the odds were in their favour. Yet now that you say so, their movements were too stiff to be well-trained fighting men."

"Did Juno send the whatever-they-were, then?" I asked. "If Snorri's right about her being a traitor, that would explain why they looked like Keepers."

"Juno outright said she wasn't affiliated with the Order at all," Aalto said. I had a vague memory of that being the case.

"That doesn't explain why the not-people that attacked us looked exactly like Keepers."

Aalto's eyes narrowed. "Something's not right here."

"Obviously," Hasebe said, wiping the blade of his wakizashi with a cleaning cloth.

"The point stands," Aalto said, his expression grave. "Creating one simulacrum takes an immense amount of skill and power, let alone nine of them. I think I need to try and get a message to Morgana directly. I have some unique channels that won't attract wide notice."

I snorted. "What, you have a cell phone?"

Aalto sighed. "Can't use one. We can't even get internet at Gladsheim faster than dial-up, thanks to the interference our magic causes."

"Snorri never mentioned that," I said, interested in spite of my weariness.

"Snorri loves to explain—to a point. I alway get the impression from the big man that he can't ever remember what all he's told any given person or other."

"He does seem to keep his cards close to his chest," I said. " Though I suppose age might be part of that. If you've outlived everyone you knew decades and centuries over, forming relationships with others might become difficult or start feeling unnecessary."

"It's something we'll have to face, too," Aalto said. "Probably not to Snorri's level, but you've met Lía. She's almost a hundred and fifty years old and barely looks a day over thirty-five. That sort of longevity creates some distance from others."

It was the first time I'd heard regret in his voice.

"I don't mean to pry," I said, "but you say that like there's a certain person you're thinking of."

Aalto was quiet for a dozen heartbeats. When he did speak up, his voice was sombre.

"Did any of your self-guided study and research tell you what a wyldmage is?"

I searched my memory. "No. The most I've ever read was a passing reference in *On Magicks and Morality*."

"That's because as rare as wizards are, wyldmagi are even fewer," Aalto said. "Many people are born with an aptitude for magic. Hell, there's an entire branch of wizard study focused on genetics and the inheritance patterns of magical talent. So many factors come into play—family history, whether or not the Lock was open when you were born, even personality in some cases."

"Rare indeed, as are the people who are born with eyes of different colours," Hasebe commented.

"Something like that. Lía aside, I've never met a single person with heterochromia. I've also never met another wizard who wasn't Drowned."

It took my brain several moments to catch the crucial word.

"*Another* wizard... so you're a wyldmage, then?"

"One of the only wyldmagi ever initiated as a full master wizard," Aalto said. "My magic awakened on its own seven years ago, a week after I turned twenty-one. My parents had no idea what happened to me. They laughed it off, thought I was just a wee bit toasty."

I paused, considering how to phrase my next question. It came out as a series of statements.

"I suppose that changed your trajectory quite a bit. I know the feeling. My father wanted me to be an economist or a model, not get a double major in clinical psychology and business."

"I was a plumber's apprentice," Aalto said. "Nearly two years in. Taking after my dad. He quit a high-power gig in Copenhagen to marry my mum and take up a quiet life as an odd job man in Aberdeen. I'm not sure either of them understood why I went off to study ancient literature with some Irish woman from Belfast."

"Do you still speak with them?" Hasebe asked, as much tenderness in his voice as I'd ever heard from him.

"I pop 'round for Christmas and holidays, when I get a chance," Aalto said, his accent thickening. "Lía ran me ragged when I was an apprentice, though. Pulled some sixteen hour days doing nothing but writing straight lines." He shivered. "I thought my hands would shrivel up."

Alto curled his fingers into wizened claws and croaked, "Your feeble skills are no match for the power of the dark side."

I chuckled, in spite of myself. "Only saw that film once."

"It's a good film. So yes, to answer your question, Hasebe. I don't know if they'll ever understand what I do, but my parents still love me and I still speak to them."

His face fell again. "Which makes it all the harder that I'll outlive them by a century or more. No one but me will even remember their names. That will be true for everyone I know who doesn't have magic."

"Can you get rid of your magic?" Hasebe asked.

Aalto shook his head. "You can let it atrophy and fall into disuse, like muscle conditioning, but it will always be there. Here's another fun fact: the law of conservation of mass applies to magic, too."

"What, you can't create or destroy magic?" I said. "No gifting power to someone else?"

"Unlike this ritual of Juno's, you can't take power from a human wizard." Aalto leaned back in his seat. "Dragons are different, apparently. But the Codex and the metaphysical structure of magic are pretty clear: no stealing power from a rival, no giving yourself magic when you don't have any to start with."

"So why are you here?" I asked. "Why do you stay if there are so many negatives?"

"Because despite the pompousness and stupid protocols and everything, I still think the Order is trying to do some good." Aalto flexed his fingers. "And even if they aren't, I'm going to."

"An honourable attitude," Hasebe said, nodding.

I had to agree. These people had not made a resoundingly positive first impression, what with their suspicion and lack of providing any solid information. The impending threat of magical lobotomy didn't make me feel any better, even though that was largely due to my previous actions.

Despite all that, Aalto had given me a glimpse into a different part of his world, one that was much more in line with my own ideas. No wonder I found him less intolerable. In another world, I could have been friends with the blue-haired wizard.

Maybe more.

My cheeks heated up as I furiously shoved the thought away.

Now is not the time, you bloody idiot. Stupid, irrational feelings have no place when the world might be about to get destroyed by your best friend.

I spun the focus ring around my index finger, mind filled of uncomfortable and awkward things for the rest of the flight.

CHAPTER FIFTEEN

A MOMENT TO BREATHE

BERGEN, NORWAY

Three days had been all it took to further turn my life upside down. I'd travelled 'round the world twice, had my heart broken by my best friend for a second time, and was beginning to feel as though Hasebe and I were running short of options.

At least I was warm enough in Scandinavia this time.

With all the globe-trotting we'd done over the last week, I'd wised up and stashed two sets of cold weather clothing in the aircar's bench seat storage during the last stopover in Knightsbridge. Snuggling into a calf-length puffer coat, I was warmed by my decision.

It had taken a few hours' travel across a few time zones to arrive in Bergen. One of the only places still open was an exclusive nightclub I was familiar with only by reputation. Out of Aalto's earshot, I gave my real name to the man at the door.

Three hours later, we were sipping aquavit at a table on the club's third floor, looking over the balcony at the dance floor below.

"How much longer are we going to give Snorri?" Aalto said, shifting in his seat. Though he fit right in amidst the club's other patrons, he looked uncomfortable.

I, on the other hand, was finally in my element. It had been too long, and I was still weary from our fight in Athens. I was more than content to stay silent and nurse my latest drink. We were far enough away from the stage that the club's ambiance was merely loud rather than bone-shaking.

"I thought you said you were going to contact the Morgana woman," Hasebe said.

"I tried," Aalto said, his voice as sharp as our drinks. "Gladsheim's emergency wards are up. That means the only means of allowed communication are through official channels. Damned magical firewalls."

"We are short on options," Hasebe said, a dark look in his eye. "It is likely the blacksmith is dead by now, despite our efforts. I do not anticipate much help will come from the old wizard."

"If Snorri's alive, he'll send help," Aalto insisted. "He wouldn't just abandon us if he knew how bad the situation had become. I just don't know how long to expect him to take."

"You are far too trusting of him," Hasebe said. "Something has been amiss about him from the start. I am beginning to suspect he may have orchestrated the attack on us in Athens."

"What possible motivation would Snorri have had to sic a group of simulacra dressed like Keepers on us?" Aalto said, glaring at Hasebe.

"The deaths of two known security risks to your precious council." Hasebe didn't break eye contact. "A move to increase his own power and station within the group."

"Murphy, I'd believe," Aalto said. "John has always struck me as the kind who'd manipulate things behind the scenes to get what he wants. But not Snorri. You couldn't pay him to be on the Althing."

"Then where is he, hm? Or does he pride himself on a lack of punctuality?"

I sighed, tearing myself away from the atmosphere.

"Gentlemen," I said, tapping the table for attention. "At this point, we need to assume it's just the three of us. If Snorri was going to send aid, he's hours too late. He knew we were coming this way."

Both men paused, turning to look at me. Neither spoke for a pair of heartbeats.

"I agree," Hasebe said, nodding. "We are being hunted by Morgana, in any case. Aid will not come from her."

Aalto frowned but didn't reply.

"Is he right?" I asked, raising an eyebrow.

"I sent Morgana a progress report before I left San Diego," Aalto replied. He made a dour face. "I hate sending updates when there's nothing to update her about."

"Which means what?"

"If she hasn't tried to reach back out at this point, wards notwithstanding, that means one of two things." Aalto held up his fingers as he talked. "Either the Althing has voted to turtle up in the castle and let the whole mess with Juno blow over... or Morgana's found out I aided you and is mustering something much nastier than the Keepers to deal with the situation. Maybe herself."

Hasebe snorted. "Too much faith and a lack of faith at the same time... it is a wonder your organisation has survived this long."

"Perhaps a stealth assault is better in any case," I said, forcing my own frustrations down. "If Ca—*Juno* caught wind that a powerful wizard such as Snorri or Morgana was bringing allies to bear against her, she could simply move early on her plan and that would be the end of it."

"An ancient, experimental piece of magical forgework can't be a speedy thing to create," Aalto said, "no matter how good Nic is. He's had a twenty-nine hour head start. Let's not lose hope just yet."

"All he was able to provide was 'south-western Norway,'" Hasebe said. He shifted in his chair, leaning across the table. "What makes you certain we are anywhere near the correct location?"

I shot a glance at Aalto to find him looking back at me. Good. That meant I wasn't the only one who'd felt it.

"Bergen isn't known for its ties to the Order," Aalto said. "As far as I know, Snorri is the only wizard who's even visited this part of Norway in the last two or three hundred years. Then again, there aren't many places Snorri doesn't visit. Anyway, feeling a pulse of magical energy in a place wizards don't hang out is a pretty good sign."

"I see. More *yokai* dealings."

"He's right, Hasebe," I said. "I felt it too. I didn't know what it was, but it's a good sign. And don't forget, there was an 'S' included in Nic's fake signature. If he did intend it to mean 'south,' Bergen is as good a place as any to start searching."

"Are you able to narrow down its source?"

I reached into my coat pocket, withdrawing a small vial full of dried blood.

"You know what this is, Hasebe. I've used it to try and find Cari before."

Finn's eyes widened. "Is that... you've a vial of her blood? How old is it?"

"Two years. It's not a great focus for any kind of location magic, but I thought it might help."

"It has not helped us before," Hasebe said, giving me an odd look.

"We didn't have access to a master wizard before."

He's behaving so oddly... what is Hasebe not telling me?

I handed the vial to Aalto, who took it gently between two fingers.

"Between this and that knife you bought from Nic, we should have a strong enough focus to narrow it down."

"Assuming either one is here." Hasebe sipped at his drink. "Are we meant to wander around Bergen until we find them?"

Finn snorted. "Magical forgework is just as much of an art as any other kind of craftsmanship. Ergo, it has a uniqueness, a signature element to it. We don't know what kind of forgework Cari is capable of, but Nic has..."

My face must have changed, despite my best efforts. Aalto trailed off, a guilty look on his face. "I'm sorry. Maybe I shouldn't call her by her real name."

I held up a hand. "No, it's alright. I nearly did it too. The two sides of her don't mesh in my mind."

Hasebe slammed his fist into the tabletop, drawing a few stares and making Aalto jump. My bodyguard stood, shame etched across his face.

"Your forgiveness, ma'am," he said in his most formal Japanese, bowing so that his forehead almost touched the table. "I have forgotten myself. It is not my place to question so fiercely these past days."

"Express your concerns, Yorimoto," I said in the same language. "But in English, so Aalto can understand."

"Very well," Hasebe said, then switched back to English. "My apologies for my outburst. It was most shameful."

"Apology accepted," Aalto said. "I'm not exactly running on all cylinders right now, either. What's the problem?"

Hasebe glanced at me, guilt and duty warring on his face.

"You continue to speak of your friend as though she has not already tried to kill you several times. There is no one side and another, no balance. There is no innocent Carissa anymore. Only Juno the wicked *yokai*."

I took another drink, playing for time.

Hasebe had yet again pointed out something I did not feel ready to address. I had believed the best of Cari for so long, even after Hasebe had saved me from a fight in our New York penthouse right before she vanished. I'd thought that had been an isolated incident, resulting from me pushing her too far.

Hasebe obviously disagreed.

"So our alternative is... what? Kill Cari?" The words leeched heat and life from the room as I spoke them.

"She tried to kill you two years ago and has nearly killed you twice more," Hasebe said. "As your head of security I cannot allow this to continue. When we find Juno again, I will put a bullet in her heart. For your sake. Your soft heart puts you in too much danger."

I didn't know what to say to that, so I kept quiet.

"Brooke?" Finn asked after a few solemn minutes.

"What do you want me to say?" I said. "You'll pardon me for struggling to turn off fifteen years of friendship."

"I must admit," Aalto said, scratching the back of his neck, "that's a new one. I can't imagine what that's like."

"You have lived so long in her shadow, you have forgotten how to exist outside it," Hasebe said. "It has been two years since she left, and all you have done since is search for her."

"So not only do we need to kill her, now I have some unhealthy, codependent relationship with my best friend?" I said. The potent alcohol was blunting all the layers of social graces I'd worked so hard my whole life to build up. After all the stress of the last few days, I was nearing my breaking point.

"I think I understand," Aalto said. He reached out and tapped the focus ring still displaying the rune sigil on my finger.

"I used to know a guy like you in secondary school. Nicest guy you'd ever meet, spent all his time worrying about other people and being there for his mates. You needed help with anything, you went to Paul."

"And?"

"Paul... killed himself halfway through his first year of uni," Aalto said. "Bottle of pills and everything. Shocked everybody who knew him. I spoke with his mum at the funeral. He left a note."

Hasebe muttered something under his breath. I caught just enough to recognize a traditional Shinto prayer for the dead.

"Are you going to tell me what the note said, or am I to guess?"

The words slipped out before I'd thought them through. I cursed myself for being so damn insensitive.

"I'm so sorry, I didn't—"

"Shut up and listen for once," Aalto said, his eyes glassy. "Paul's final note only had ten words in it. He said, 'I have nothing left. I gave everything I had away.'"

I kept quiet. He continued on.

"My point is, you've given a lot of your life and friendship and time and energy to this girl. Best friends are amazing treasures, don't get me wrong. But you can't define yourself by how you relate to one person. You're a caretaker, I can see that. I suspect you acted like everybody's mum when you were younger."

"That would explain my interest in psychology and behavioural disorders," I said. My voice quavered.

"Your identity has to come from objective reality, not things you think are true about yourself." Aalto tapped the table for emphasis. "And it can't come from your relationship to Cari. Paul's last words have stuck with me for going on nine years now. You can't get so focused on saving others that you forget to save yourself."

I swallowed past the lump of icy charcoal in my throat, looking back and forth between the two men. I'd heard Hasebe's perspective many times, more still in just the past week. Aalto's thoughts were something I hadn't taken time to consider until now.

What was my life, really?

I had interests, certainly, but most of those had been cultivated as opposition to my father. They were things I enjoyed, though not entirely things I'd perhaps have chosen to do if not for him. Those were fairly significant choices I'd made not for myself, in other words.

My graduate degree was another one. I did have an interest in understanding the human brain and what makes it work, but Cari had been so miserable after the summer in Bristol I'd chosen to pursue a graduate degree in psychology in an attempt to learn how I could help her. Strike two for choices made because of someone else.

Hasebe was right. Finn was right.

I'd spent so long living my life for other people I'd neglected myself entirely. Even that thought felt selfish and arrogant. I'd have to spend some time with this. Perhaps I'd need to have Westaway take me on a long drive in the old Bentley once this matter was settled.

Then a thought struck me, unrelated to my soul-searching.

"Who was driving the car?"

Both men gave me confused looks.

"What car?" Aalto asked.

"Juno kidnapped Nic and got away in a car that night in San Diego," I said. "But she couldn't have driven the car. It showed up while we were in a standoff with her. Even remote-pilot cars don't work that well in the dark."

"And if Juno really has that much raw magical power, remote-pilot wouldn't have worked regardless," Aalto said, comprehension dawning in his eyes. "The stronger your magic is, the worse its interference with complex technology."

"So Juno has an accomplice," Hasebe said. "That explains a great deal."

"Did your reports say anything about her having an accomplice?" I asked, turning to Aalto.

He shook his head. "All Snorri had was her body type and her codename. He's been assembling a profile on her for almost six months."

I stood up, stumbling backwards in my haste.

"Juno has a leak on the inside," I said. "If she's not a former member of the Order, that's the only thing that makes sense."

Aalto's face paled. "And if Snorri went back to Gladsheim to get help..."

"We must hurry," Hasebe said.

Aalto slapped down a pair of bills on our table as Hasebe and I strode out of the bar.

Chapter Sixteen

TWIST THE KNIFE

A n hour later we had driven our rented car to the southern side of Bergen, near the waterfront. It reminded me of days earlier in Reykjavik, though this time the sun hadn't yet peeked over the horizon. The industrial buildings and warehouses weren't as old and weathered as the Icelandic city had been, but the smell was almost identical.

Through a hurried bit of magic, my antler-handled knife had led us to one of the smaller warehouses in this area, an old brick building wedged between two modern-looking ones. That was all we were able to see in the light from the car's headlamps. Hasebe and I rolled our windows down, letting in the gentle sounds of the early morning along with the growl of the car's engine. I'd rested just long enough to feel some of my magical strength return. It would have to be enough.

I tapped into my magical senses, focused on the building, and dry-heaved. I'd never sensed such an overwhelming, buzzing *cold* before.

So many wards... I can't even sense any seams or individual workings.

"Place feels like a fortress," Aalto said, his jaw set. "I think this is it. Only surprise is the lack of sentries."

"Probably doesn't need them—it's warded to the moon and back. How do we get past that?" I still felt short of breath after the brief mental touch. "I can't even tell what all is there, only that it's there."

"There is always a weakness," Hasebe said. "No matter how hard you try to shore up against it."

I reached out again with my farsight, setting my teeth as the sensations flooded in again. There was an odd emotional resonance to the place, which became less muddled the deeper I searched. It resolved into a fierce sense of pride, much the same as Nic's workshop exuded. Mingled with pride was iron hard determination that would crush a mountain if it stood in its way.

Underneath both of those was something familiar—an old, old sense of loneliness. I'd sensed that in only one person before.

"Aalto, we may have a problem," I said, pushing deeper towards that last feeling. I needed to be sure, because if I was...

—a tired old man sits on top of a boulder looking over the valley far below He knows he's the only one left and it never gets easier The ache inside him grows day by day but he has to keep going He must become stronger Strong enough to—

"Yes?" Aalto said, breaking me out of the experience.

I shuddered, releasing my farsight. That had confirmed my fears. The cold feeling settled in my stomach.

"Do you know how to get around Snorri's defences?"

Hasebe snarled a curse in Japanese. "I knew it!"

Aalto's dark eyes widened. "You can't be serious. How can you—"

"I felt it, alright?" I pointed out the window at the brick building. "Farsight is the one thing I can do well and this place screams of Snorri. We need to get in there. Now."

My voice hardened as I spoke, turning me into the iron lady my father always wanted me to be. That brought its own mix of emotional mud.

"Can a single hex rune break through that many wards?" I asked.

Aalto's mouth snapped shut and he coughed. "Yeah! Yeah. Well, no. Not unless it's very powerful. Typically you'd start with a foundation rune, and..." he trailed off, digging in his coat pocket. "Hang on. I've got some chalk."

Hasebe pulled the car up into the alley beside the little brick building. Aalto and I got out.

"I'll draw the circle," he said, sketching two perfect circles on the pavement, one inside the other. "You draw the runes."

"Suggestions?" I knew which runes could do what, but Finn was a master. Might as well take advantage of his knowledge.

"Start with Berkana, not more than nine times. Attach Fehu and Jera to bind it together."

I began drawing the runes - angular capital 'B', an 'F' with the tines bent up, and two right angles almost touching each other. Aalto watched, offering comments here and there. He was as efficient as I'd suspected and a quite good teacher on top of that.

Once the circle was made and all the runes chalked on the pavement, Aalto gestured to Hasebe. My bodyguard left the car running but stepped out with a silenced pistol drawn. I powered off my phone and pulled out the antler-hilted knife I'd bought from Nic, holding it with the flat edge pressed against my forearm.

This was it. Time to see if my magic was really all that strong.

I stepped into the circle, drawing up my power to close it. The air around me chilled several degrees. Imagining the rune I wanted, an uppercase 'N' shape, I slashed out with the knife clutched in my left hand and hissed, "*Hagalaz!*"

The invisible circle of power flared once. A wave of energy swept through me, burning with an icy fire I'd never felt before. I'd expected to fall unconscious again, but my power surged through the binding and foundation runes I'd inscribed. The circle took the brunt of the effort, amplifying the rune I'd spoken aloud at least ninefold. The hex rune was brilliant at destroying technology, hence turning off my phone. I had no idea what it would do against Snorri's wards.

Bolts of lightning arced out from the brick wall, revealing ghostly afterimages of runes carved into their surfaces. Sparks flew as one of the transformers overhead shorted out, plunging the area into even deeper darkness. A clap of thunder cut through the night, with one final electrical discharge almost striking the car.

Hasebe fired two silenced rounds into the wooden front door's lock and kicked it open. The door slammed against the inside wall, knob clattering to the tiled floor.

I smudged the chalk circle with my foot, letting its power flow away harmlessly into the sidewalk. Aalto got to the door just before I did. We entered the workshop at almost the same time.

At first glance, it was a small, ordinary house. We'd burst into the dining and kitchen area, with two doors leading elsewhere. The first led to the bathroom, but through the second was a room similar to Nic's workshop. Bookshelves dominated one wall and a thick workbench sat in the centre of the room, while shelves on a second wall were filled with containers of bits and bobs.

Nic's workshop hadn't smelled like old blood, though. Nor had it contained a set of chains against the far wall with a bloodied figure slumped in them.

"Nic!" Aalto shouted, racing across the room.

Hasebe emerged from another room, gun held in both hands. "He isn't here. Nor is she."

"Nic is," I said. "Quickly. We need to see if he's still alive."

We hurried across the room. Aalto was fussing with the cuffs, his teeth bared in a snarl.

"Bastard," he said. "Why would anyone do this to a person?"

Nic coughed, his chest heaving as he took a breath. I glanced around, eyes roaming the room for a pair of bolt cutters or some such.

Hasebe stepped past me and ripped one chain out of the wall with his cybernetic hand, breaking it.

"I didn't know you could do that," I said.

"Overclock," Hasebe replied, flexing his mechanical fingers. "It is like giving my limb a burst of electric adrenaline. I cannot do it for long."

He tore the second chain loose from the wall. Nic collapsed forward onto Aalto. I knelt down next to them.

Nic looked a mess. Aside from ragged clothes, his face was bloody, one eye swollen shut. I thought his nose might have been broken. One of his wrists was swollen beneath the handcuffs and his opposite shoulder had an ugly line seared into it. More bruises and burn marks streaked his chest and upper thighs, burning one nipple off completely.

Anger built up inside me. Had Cari done this? Or had it been Snorri?

"Hasebe," I said, turning. "Did you see any medicinal herbs or such while you were clearing rooms? Mugwort, ashwagandha, anything?"

"No, but I was not looking for them," he admitted.

I shot up and hurried to the kitchen. My luck came through in the fifth cabinet I opened. Jars with labels in a blocky handwriting stood on the bottom shelf. I grabbed the three that would be most useful and dashed back.

Someone had gotten Nic a chair and seated the Valdisson on it. Aalto whispered a word, projecting a small, glowing orb above Nic's head. It made his wounds look that much worse.

"...is worse than you can imagine," Nic croaked as I approached. "The girl isn't the one in charge."

"She's got an accomplice, we know," I said, unscrewing the lid from one jar. "Chew on this mugwort. It'll lessen the pain and begin healing. We don't have time to make a proper poultice. I'm sorry."

"I've felt worse," Nic said, forced nonchalance in his voice as he took the clump of leaves I offered. "But we need to hurry. The plan has been moved up. You've got them worried, little raven."

I thought I was the dove...?

"Where are they going?" Aalto asked. "Did you hear?"

Nic hissed in a breath, adjusting himself on the chair. "A magical place, obviously. There are several places like that in the world. Tahiti, for instance."

Frustrating as it was, I had to admire the man's glibness in spite of his injuries and what he'd just endured. Rebellion was a state of mind I understood all too well.

"Perhaps a better question is whether or not you succeeded, master smith," Hasebe said.

Nic managed to assemble his battered features into an expression of wounded pride. "Of course I succeeded in forging the Open Chain. I wouldn't be alive if I hadn't."

"We need to get him to a hospital," I said. "I can't do much more for him with just these herbs."

Aalto let out a frustrated growl. "We still don't know where Snorri and Juno are going. Again."

"That's not Snorri."

Both of us turned to look down at Nic. The man spread his fingers, as much as he could do without moving his arms.

"Rather, it is Snorri Sturluson, but that's not truly who he is. That identity has been his disguise for only the last eight hundred years, if I'm right."

"Who is he, then?" I asked.

Nic swallowed, his face twisting in pain. "Snorri's true identity is Odin. The Allfather. The wisest and most powerful battle-mage of all the Aesir."

Blood drained from my face. "Oh."

This had indeed just gotten worse.

⋘ᚾ⋙

We got Nic settled into the backseat of the rental car moments before he passed out. With no way to get his cuffs off, our options were either scour the house for the key and risk angering yet another police force or simply leave them on for the time being. We elected to leave and avoid possible confrontation, Hasebe taking us a back way towards the edge of Bergen.

"How's he holding up?" Aalto asked, turning around in his seat to look at us.

"Pulse is there, but he's lost a lot of blood," I said, wrapping more bandages around his torso. "At least a broken wrist and a possible skull fracture, too. I can't be certain what else is damaged, but... it's bad."

Finn's dark eyes said he wanted to question my certainty, but he chose not to. A wise move, considering the circumstances. I was seething.

I didn't have much of a connection to Nic, to be sure, but the brief MediMerge training I'd been through a decade ago hadn't prepared me to aid a man nearly beaten to death.

I sincerely hope this wasn't Cari's work. If she's done this... maybe there is no hope after all.

I shook away the dark thought and focused back on Nic's wounds.

"Odin," Aalto mused. "You know, that makes a lot of sense. It explains all the weird nonsense he's been able to do since I've known him."

I thought back to the ghostly *fylgja* bear Snorri had called up in London, which he'd said was an ancient and rare art.

"So it would seem," I said. "If he is truly over a thousand years old, no wonder he's gone batty."

I paused. "He's also probably the one that fed Ca—*Juno* all her information. No wonder she always seemed a step ahead. He's known the whole time what's going on."

"Why would they have revealed such a valuable piece of information to the smith?" Hasebe asked. "More relevant, if he completed the Chain, why did they leave him in Bergen alive?"

"I'm right here, you know. Just dozed off." Nic let out a deep sigh.

"Then answer my question," Hasebe said.

"Well, as to the first point, I, ah... may have goaded the big man into punching me in the face. Wasn't hard, really. He'd found out about the Westin Northwaitte note somewhere along the way. Nasty right hook, Odin had. Made him think he'd knocked me unconscious. That led to a big argument where much of this was revealed. He would have finished me off after that, as well... had it not been for Juno."

"What?" I turned to stare at Nic.

"God's honest truth," Nic said, crossing himself. The bandages I'd put around his right arm limited his motion, but the gesture was clear.

"I expected her to be all for it, but she talked him down. Said it would be a waste of future resources, since I provably had the skills to craft the Open Chain."

"That seems out of character," Aalto said. "Juno's been so violent every time we've encountered her."

"She's also run away every time we've encountered her," I said. A spark of hope flickered in my chest. "Maybe she's not all the way gone."

"Utilitarian does not mean good, Brooke," Aalto said. "I'm all for giving second chances and taking risks, believe me. Even if she was your friend, Juno is still willingly going along with—and maybe instigating—a ritual that requires a human sacrifice. That's one of the darkest things you can do with magic, and you can't do things with magic you don't believe in. Deciding to keep a useful person alive means nothing."

Try as I would, I couldn't assemble a counterargument. Pragmatism and friendship warred inside me again. I so desperately didn't want my best friend to be gone, but facts were hard to contest.

Nic spoke up again. "You're right about the ritual, but there's another facet to consider. If Odin and Juno both knew the ritual needed a sacrifice, by all rights they should have taken me with them regardless of Juno's pragmatism. Why didn't they?"

"It would not be difficult for ones with such lack of honour and morality to kidnap another victim," Hasebe said from the driver's seat.

"Unless one of them doesn't know about that part of the ritual," Aalto said. "Is that what you're getting at, Nic?"

"Yes," Nic said. "Loki may be the well-known, mischievous liar in folklore, but Odin is not without his own powers of disguise and deception. Think of how he connived his way into gaining the Mead of Poetry."

A horrible thought exploded in my brain like a bolt of lightning.

"You're saying *Cari* is the sacrifice?"

"Unwilling, maybe," Nic said. "But yes. Juno, or Cari, or whatever her name is, could very well play the part of victor and victim here."

"And if he's truly Odin, of course she'd go along with him," I said, coldness spreading through my chest. "He could lie to her and manipulate her so easily by preying on her love of mythology. She has a doctorate in it, for God's sake. Why would he need to find another sacrificial lamb if one comes trotting up to him?"

I realised with a start that the cold feeling wasn't fear for my best friend.

It was fury.

"And if he fed her some line about binding and killing Nidhogg for the role it plays in causing Ragnarök," Aalto said, "he might have even convinced her she's helping save the world. Damn, that's clever. He gets to take down one of his greatest fears and increase his own powers at the same time."

"Odin will die," I said, speaking my anger to life. "By my hand, if need be."

The focus ring on my finger flared with blue-green light. I covered it with my other hand.

"We don't even know where he is," Aalto said, slumping against his seat. "All we have to go on is 'someplace magical.' There are dozens of magical places in the world."

"Unfortunate, but true," Nic added. "Not to mention the fact that he's Odin, Brooke."

"I don't care," I said, clenching my left fist. Sparks of magical energy flickered between my fingers. "If there's even half a chance you're right about her being the victim in this mad ritual, I have to save Cari."

"I do not want to admit it," Hasebe said, words coming slowly, "but she is our greatest weapon against Odin. If we can convince her."

Aalto raised an eyebrow. "What would make Juno take our word over his?"

I thought I saw where Hasebe was going with this and gave him a grateful nod. "Cari killed her ex-boyfriend two years ago to avenge the abuse she suffered at his hands. Due to that and some other trauma, she has some trust issues with men. Seeing one of her mythological heroes come to life may have made her ignore any red flags that would have raised for her otherwise. But if we can get her to question Odin, even just a little..."

"Not to mention the sacrifice part of the ritual," Nic said. "If I were her, I wouldn't be very happy with someone trying to use me like that."

"Precisely," Hasebe said. "All we need her to do is turn against Odin. That may prove unexpected enough to win the day."

I noticed what he had left unsaid—just precisely what we'd do with Cari once Odin was down. Or if that approach failed.

"Seems like our best shot," Aalto said. "But I remind you again, we don't know where they've—"

Hasebe swerved, barking something impolite. A figure stood in the road, cloak flapping in the wind.

At the same time, the image of a moonlit beach flared through my mind. Waves lapped at the dark sand, reflecting the full moon overhead. The shadows of tall, dead trees fell over the beach, obscuring most other details.

The image moved, as though I'd turned my head. A craggy face stared back at me, one eye covered by a black patch. The other eye was a shining gold colour.

"Brooke?"

I shot back to reality, vision returned to normal. Aalto was staring at me.

"I know where she is," I said, excitement creeping into my voice. "I know where they are."

"We've got a more immediate problem," Aalto said, his eyes flicking past me out the window. I followed his gaze. Several figures in green cloaks were approaching the car.

It clicked half a second later. "More fake Keepers?"

"I'd prefer that. These guys are for real. I recognise one of them."

"Nine enemies," Hasebe said from the drivers' seat.

"We don't have time for this," I said, unbuckling my seatbelt. "I know where Cari and Odin are. We have to go."

"You step out there, you're dead," Aalto said, grabbing my shoulder. "I don't think we can talk our way out of this one. Or at least, you can't."

I clenched my teeth, but some pesky facts and logic backed up his statement. Hasebe and I had been running from the Keepers for several days now. We'd likely get ourselves killed sooner than reason with them. I had no choice but to trust Aalto again and hope he'd get the four of us out of this.

CHAPTER SEVENTEEN

DESPERATE MEASURES

Under the watchful eye of the other Keepers and their flintlocks, Hasebe and I were disarmed and placed in handcuffs as we knelt on the side of the road. The woman responsible didn't look any older than me, but with wizards that wasn't saying sweet FA.

Aalto was forced at gunpoint to help extract Nic from the back of the rental car, where another of the Keepers began tending to his injuries.

"How horrible," he said, words twisted by an accent much like Snorri's. "I can't imagine anyone doing this to another person."

"At least I'm not dead," Nic replied, wincing as the Keeper medic wrapped another roll of bandage around his chest. "If it does anything for her case, the young lady over there did a fair job patching me up before you arrived."

I shot him an appreciative look.

"That'll be for the Althing to decide," the medic replied, glancing back at his colleagues.

"I'm on the Althing, half-wit," Aalto snapped, flipping hair out of his face as he glared at the Keeper who seemed to be in charge. The man looked middle-aged, his dark hair and beard cropped close.

He sighed. "We showed up to verify an unusual burst of warding energies being released in southwestern Norway. Instead I find a renegade wizard and two fugitives along with a Valdisson nearly beat to death. The Althing means nothing at this point. No one is untouchable."

"I'm damn sure I outrank Murphy," Aalto said. "He's the one who sent you here, isn't he?"

"If you must know, we received a report from Snorri Sturluson that something strange was happening."

"So when Sturluson says jump, you just do it?" I glared at the Keepers. "He's not even on your bloody council!"

I was rewarded with a backhanded slap across the face for my trouble.

"Not a word, *seidhkona*," the female Keeper said, adjusting her combat gloves. "Things are going to go badly enough for you already."

Hasebe growled, his eyes burning. I was certain he would've broken his handcuffs and snapped the woman's neck if it would've gotten me out of there. I held him back with a look. Now was not the time. These were not the same mindless creatures we d dispatched back in Athens.

I can't believe we thought those were real... the differences are so stark.

"Leave her be," Aalto snapped, taking a step towards me. One of the others brandished his flintlock. Aalto stopped, raising both hands.

"Look, there's been a big misunderstanding here," he said. "These two have nothing to do with Juno or the thefts. Hell, they've been helping me try to stop her for the last few days!"

"And ignoring a direct instruction to return to Gladsheim to do so," the head Keeper said, gesturing at me. "She was supposed to be brought in and sworn to the Codex as a potential security risk."

"You can't forcibly conscript me against my will," I said. "I've no intention of going around spilling magical secrets I don't even know."

"It's standard procedure, Miss Gilkeson," the man replied. "Otherwise our opposites and other magical beings might try to use you as leverage to get to the Order. It's happened before."

"It won't matter a lick if you don't let us go," I said, drawing up as much grace and poise as I could. "Juno has an extremely powerful accomplice and could very well destroy the world if we don't stop her. Immediately."

"You should listen," Nic said. "The girl is right."

"That's a matter for us, not you," the female Keeper replied, turning toward him. "Our instructions are to get these two back to the castle and let the Althing sort them out."

"I'm on the bloody—" Aalto sighed, running a hand through his hair before straightening to his full height. "I am Finn Aalto, Seventh of the Opened Lock. As master wizard and a member of the High Althing, I order you to release these two prisoners to my personal custody."

The Keepers all paused for a second, several exchanging glances. I hadn't realised Aalto carried quite so much clout.

For a moment, I thought that would be enough.

The lead Keeper threw back his hood, running a hand over his buzzed hair. "Councilor Aalto, I'm sorry. I know that's an official request, and I'm not trying to be difficult. Not only is this standard procedure, my instructions came directly from Morgana herself."

Aalto rocked back a step. "What?"

"One of our contacts in Athens sent in a telegram yesterday regarding the discovery of several magically decomposing creatures dressed as Keepers," the lead Keeper said. "The other captains and myself were ordered by Morgana and Snorri Sturluson to be on high alert for any suspicious discharges of power. We were also warned that there could be a Loki-kin at work."

"A shape-changer?" Nic said. "I'd be surprised. I slew one of the last two in 1931."

The female Keeper's eyes widened above her combat scarf. She looked down at me. "For a renegade, you keep some impressive company."

I sighed. "That doesn't make me feel better."

However Snorri had summoned or sent those fake Keepers after us, it was proving to be almost as disruptive as if they'd actually killed us. And if he'd truly gotten to Morgana, it wouldn't matter what we said or did. We'd lost before even beginning to fight.

I decided to play my last card.

"Odin is involved in this mess," I told the Keeper. "He's helping Juno conduct a summoning ritual with dire consequences if it goes awry. You have to release us. We know where he's going to do it."

"Odin?" The female Keeper laughed. "He hasn't been seen in the wild since the end of the Second World War. He's likely dead by now."

"The girl's right," Aalto and Nic said at the same time.

"He's the one responsible for this," Nic added, gesturing at himself. "You think either of those two could have hurt me this badly?"

Hasebe huffed. I was beginning to feel his agitation. This whole dialogue was getting us nowhere. We had more important things to do. Cari could still be saved if we hurried.

"*Extraction,*" I signed, twitching my fingers out of sight of the Keepers. "*Call Westaway?*"

"GPS chip is on," Hasebe replied in kind. *"Minutes if ready."*

"Wait for signal."

I glanced up to find Aalto looking at me. The female Keeper didn't seem to have noticed the coded conversation with Hasebe, fixated instead on Nic.

"Nic, how do you feel?" Aalto said, not breaking eye contact with me.

"Not as bad as I did an hour ago," he said, waving the medic away. "I can probably walk a few steps."

"We took a Bridge to get here," the lead Keeper said. "I didn't know we'd need to transport anyone. Apologies, Valdisson, but you'll have to walk a fair way."

"I don't think that will be a problem," Nic said, glancing at Finn. "I'm already feeling much better."

Aalto's eyes continued to burn into mine, as if he were searching for something. I stared back, willing him to sense my desperation. His shoulders tensed, and the muscles in his jaw bunched.

The blue-haired wizard sighed. "I'm really sorry about this, ladies and gents."

The lead Keeper's head snapped up. "Councillor? What are you—"

"Laguz!"

Aalto snapped both wrists out to his sides, engulfing the small area in a cloud of damp fog. I could just make out the tensed form of my bodyguard inches to the left.

A small LED flared violet in Hasebe's cybernetic forearm. The sounds of snapping metal followed seconds later, then a gurgling feminine cough. The prone form of the female Keeper landed in front of me, a huge knot forming on her forehead.

I struggled to my feet, still bound by the handcuffs. A guttural howl tore through the fog, which swirled as Hasebe lunged into the group of Keepers.

Which one of us is truly the yokai, *I wonder?*

"Isa," I whispered, pulling my wrists taut against the cuffs. Focused by the ring on my finger, magical energy surged through my left arm, freezing the cuff solid. It snapped, leaving a pair of tiny cuts on either side of my wrist.

"Non-lethal only!" Aalto's voice barked through the fog. He gave a grunt of effort, then added, "Nic, let's go!"

Someone grabbed my wrist, pulling me out of the fog. I thought it was Hasebe until I looked up to see the lead Keeper glaring at me.

"I don't want to hurt you," he said, "but I will. Don't resist."

To hell with it. I've faffed about enough with these people.

I lashed up with my knee, catching him between the legs. As the lead Keeper curled protectively toward his nethers I shoved hard against his chest, sending the man stumbling backwards into the fog.

Before he could react, I turned and sprinted towards the rental car. A lance of fire blasted past my head out of the fog cloud, melting a hole straight through the car's windscreen as it splattered against the leather seat. I pulled up short, glancing around for the others.

Nic flopped against the car's bonnet on the other side, grinning weakly at me. "I trust you have a plan to get us out of here?"

"Do you have any magic left?"

He nodded. "I hurt but my reserves are deep. What do you need?"

"Amplification circle," I barked. "Small and potent as you can make it. I don't have much magic left."

"You are learning," Nic said, his grin widening. He drew a cracked fingernail through the paint on the car's bonnet, scrawling a circle of runes.

"Not getting that rental deposit back," I muttered, drawing up another scrap of my power. Despite the speed, Nic's angled lines were perfect. He'd given me two elegant rings of circles filled with runes. Even without my power to focus it, the circle shimmered with potential magic.

Aalto had used the water rune to create a fog cloud moments before. It was a good idea, but I had something a little chillier in mind.

"Aalto! Hasebe!" I shouted, knowing full well I was giving away my position. If this didn't work, we were screwed. "Clear the fog!"

Hasebe barked an acknowledgement in Japanese. I couldn't wait for Aalto.

"Isa!" I said, slamming my left hand into the circle Nic had carved. The bonnet's thin metal dented under the blow. Light flared through the runes, releasing the working of my power into reality as a fresh wave of fatigue raced through me.

Ice crystals blossomed around the seven figures still in the cloud of fog. Aalto rolled backwards just in time to avoid the trap as the Keepers' cloaks and clothing froze solid.

The growling whine of repulsor engines in the sky drew my attention. I scanned the horizon and made out an expanding black ellipse drawing closer to us. Westaway was imminent.

"Hasebe!" I called, glancing around for him. Motion drew my eye to the left. My bodyguard was atop the lead Keeper and had just landed a solid—thankfully human—fist to the side of his neck. That done, he straightened and jogged over to where Nic and I huddled by the car.

"Clever," he said, surveying the immobilised Keepers. "Uncomfortable, but not deadly. Perhaps there is hope for these *yokai* tactics after all."

"That was me, Hasebe," I said, breathless.

My bodyguard gave me a wolfish grin. "Then you have been paying attention. Let's go."

Aalto shook his head. "I mean nothing against any of you," he said to the group of frozen Keepers. "I will explain later, you have my word."

The downdraft from the repulsor's engines stirred our coats as Westaway settled to the road behind the rental car. It rocked on its axles but stayed put, thankfully. I jumped before the aircar's side hatch was fully open, clearing it with a roll that smacked my back into the opposite door. Hasebe came next, extending a hand to help Nic into the aircar.

"Aalto!" I called, limbs shaking. "We have to go. Let's move!"

I wasn't sure if he'd heard me over the engines, but soon enough Aalto made a bow-legged dash into the aircar. "I'm aboard."

"Westaway!" I called toward the cockpit mic. "Set sat-nav for Bristol Harbour."

Everyone in the passenger lounge stared at me.

"Bristol?" Aalto said. "What the hell is in—"

"It's the closest place to that island," I said. "She's at the Lock."

CHAPTER EIGHTEEN

PLAN OF ATTACK

I n all the confusion, none of us had thought to stop and reclaim our weapons—none of us save Aalto. He'd shoved as much as he could fit in his trousers and legged it.

Hasebe's eyes widened just slightly at the sight of his frost-coated Cobalt. From his boot, Aalto withdrew my antler-hilt knife. I gave him a grateful nod, slipping the knife back in its sheath. It was all I could manage.

In a few moments, Hasebe had his travel arsenal back together. He nodded his thanks.

"What makes you so sure they're at the Lock?" Aalto asked, sinking into the bench seat next to Nic. "It's a huge gamble if you're wrong."

I glanced across at him. "I'm not wrong. I saw her."

Nic's eyebrows raised. "I know you have potential, but you're a bit young for your farsight to be working like that. Are you certain?"

Finn glanced from Nic to me.

I sighed. "Alright, I didn't exactly see Cari. I saw what she saw, through her eyes. Snorri was there."

Nic whistled. "That's a special kind of bond-sight. No one's expressed that power since the Ninth cycle, and I was just a boy then. We do live in interesting times."

Aalto's face went blank, an expression I knew quite well. He'd just realised something but didn't want to give it away. I was too tired to press him on it, which meant our conversation ended there.

With Westaway flying all-out, we touched down in Bristol's Floating Harbour around half-six in the morning. I spent most of the journey interrogating Aalto and Nic about enchanting, while Hasebe checked and loaded weapons he pulled from a cache I hadn't known was in the aircar.

We needed stealth and speed for our assault on the island, qualities that often conflicted with each other. Nic had also warned that trying to do any kind of strong magic inside the aircar might interfere with its electronic systems.

Having seen the aftermath of several smartphones in the wake of powerful magic, I had to agree. I also didn't fancy being shot out of the sky by a fireball as soon as we crested the horizon, even if the magic hadn't been a problem. The aerial approach was fast, but wouldn't do us much good in this situation.

That meant getting creative.

The *Margaret Ann,* my father's luxury catamaran, floated just above the surface of the River Avon in its private marina. Even powered down, its top-grade repulsor engines kept the twin-hulled craft from touching the water. I'm told that's to do with drag and aerodynamics and such.

Vaulting onto the deck, I took the spare key stub from its hiding spot under the nav console and brought the hoverboat's systems online.

"This won't interfere with the illusion, will it?" I asked as Nic unrolled a small belt of engraving tools. "I know the aircar was out, but this 'boat is still quite techy."

The Valdisson knelt down beside me, examining the equipment. "Repulsor engines have been around long enough for the magic to get used to them. It usually takes a few decades or so for magic to catch up. Navigation may be harder, though. Satellites are too new."

I nodded. "I've got these coordinates memorised. You do what you need to."

"This is incredible!" Aalto said, jumping onto the deck. "I've never seen a car this swish, let alone a hoverboat."

"We've had it for over a decade now," I said. "That's Palaeolithic for rich people."

"You say that like you'd rather not be one," Nic commented.

"I have a complex relationship with my financial status," I said. "Does the 'boat need to be powered off for you to start?"

"Runecanting of this sort..." Nic scratched the stubble on his chin. "No, I don't think so. If there's going to be interference with my working, better that I know what it is right from the start."

I nodded, tapping the nav console. Displays and diagnostic panels came to life, bathing the deck in a soothing teal glow. A soft hum underscored Nic's work as he pulled out a scoring tool along with several bits and bobs I didn't recognize.

"The key to a masking glamour," he said, "is to make it as real as possible. Sounds simple, I know, but Jerica has a habit of making her illusions a little too perfect. That's when it dips into the uncanny valley and spoils the surprise."

"Do well, not perfect," I said. "Not the message I ever got as a child."

Nic snorted, shaking his head as Hasebe helped him sit down on the deck. I pulled the catamaran out into the river as Nic worked, steering towards the mouth of the river and the Celtic Sea.

"I don't suppose you stowed any extra weapons onboard?" Aalto asked, sitting in one of the deck chairs behind me.

I shot Hasebe a look, but my bodyguard's expression remained stoic. "We haven't used this vessel in over a year. I thought it unnecessary."

"Fair enough," Aalto said. "But the more unexpected we can be with our assault, the better."

"Wizards don't seem all that bulletproof," I said.

Hasebe chuckled.

"I've seen a couple put up some damn good shield wards against bullets," Aalto said. "Thing is, with wards you have to know the attack is coming. Putting a ward up in the middle of a fight versus having one up from the start makes a huge difference."

"So if I shot Odin in the back when his wards were unprepared," Hasebe said, "he would die?"

I resisted needling my bodyguard for how dishonourable that sort of attack seemed. Our opponent was much too dangerous for that. Not to mention I'd put the poor man through enough tests of his loyalty, what with everything I'd asked him to overlook the past few days. I'd have to make it up to Hasebe if we survived this.

"Aim for the head," Aalto said. "If I've learned anything from watching the Keepers at work, it's that combat-focused wizards and battlemages have a strange aversion to headgear."

"Too many action movies," Hasebe said, his lip curling in disgust. "I would have all of us in body armour for this if there were time."

Aalto chuckled. "Anyhow, we need to be prepared for their response. We've got so many stories and legends about Odin's fighting capabilities it's not even funny. No wonder people thought he was a god."

I inhaled a long, slow breath. "We do have one small advantage. Cari's favourite power is useless here because we all know how the Suggestion illusion works."

"I don't," Hasebe said. "How am I to protect myself?"

"By being on guard against it," Finn said. "The only way that form of illusion can work on a strong-willed person without magic is for them to be caught unawares."

"That explains the thing in the library," I said under my breath. Cari had successfully convinced the terrorist's ringleader not to notice her weeks before the attack, but the same Suggestion hadn't worked during our final skirmish with him. He'd been too prepared the second time.

"Expect her to try and use it on you, Hasebe," I said. "You and I both know how stubborn she is."

My bodyguard nodded. "For your sake, I will make Odin the priority. I think it is unwise to do so."

"Noted. I'm going to try and talk Cari down. Perhaps that's foolhardy, I don't know. I can't give up on her."

"Can you feel the good in her?" Finn quipped. When I glared at him, he winced. "Sorry. I get mouthy when I'm anxious."

I snorted. "*This* is what's making you anxious? Not anything else we've done this week?"

An electric ripple of magic washed over the catamaran. Its repulsor engines growled in protest for a second before stabilising back to their normal pitch.

"That's it!" Nic said, collapsing onto the deck. His olive complexion was a shade or two lighter. "The working is up and running."

"Are you alright?" I asked, glancing down at the smith.

He nodded. "Took more out of me than it usually does. I'll need to rest for a week or two when this is over."

If there is an after.

I shook that thought away and focused on piloting the catamaran.

After a few seconds, I realised what was missing. Any noise that the 'boat itself made, from engines to creaking sounds as it shifted in the water, were gone. Wisps of grey drifted across my field of vision, enough that I thought I was losing consciousness.

"Nic?" I said, lowering my voice. "Will our voices carry through the illusion?"

"I've masked the sound and image of the hoverboat," he replied. "The image won't stand up to close inspection, but I had enough bottled silence left over from the chain to craft a top-shelf muffling illusion."

"That explains the visuals, but you haven't answered my question."

He tilted his head in what was almost a nod. "It should, but I'd be cautious."

I closed my eyes, turning back to the control board.

The island, which I'd never found on a map and still had no name for, peeked over the horizon about ten minutes later. I made out the outlines of the jagged sea stacks on its southern shore, still raw and scraped in some places. My heart fluttered.

"Four lives, forever impacted by this place," I murmured.

This was where I'd Drowned eight years ago, where my magic and other gifts had first made themselves known. Amy and Cari had been similarly changed here, though they hadn't Drowned on the island proper.

Besides the magic, that shipwreck had also been the beginning of the end for Cari and her second boyfriend—the good one. In her worse moments, Cari had often blamed the island for ruining her life.

As a sick feeling settled in my stomach, I thought I finally understood.

I focused inward, searching for my magic. The well of power inside me sparkled, sending a tingling sensation through my left arm. That was good. Between the aircar flight and this brief journey I'd rested more than expected. Nic and Finn's focusing runes had been quite efficient, too, keeping me from passing out like Jerica had in San Diego.

I tried to ignore the fact that I had started thinking of the blue-haired wizard on a first name basis and turned my attention to strategising. If I was able to calm Cari down enough to attempt reason... no, that wouldn't do. I'd have to appeal to her sense of paranoia. Our past friendship didn't seem to mean much to her, so perhaps self-preservation would be a better approach.

I looked inside once again, calling up images of the runes I'd seen in Gladsheim. Sowilo, my self-healing rune, came first. The angular shape of the force rune, Uruz, came to mind next, followed by Laguz, the water rune. It wasn't a great deal, but the focus ring would help make that little I had useful.

Thunder crackled overhead. I glanced up to see grey clouds rolling over the sea, darkening the sky around them. The sound brought with it a flash of inspiration. A smile touched my lips. I'd keep that in my pocket for now, but it was reassuring to know I had something else to help.

Finn approached with a Sharpie, gesturing for my hand. I held it out to him, the marker's tip tickling my skin as he drew the communication rune on the back of my hand. A tingle of magic surrounded the rune, prickling like lidocaine. A few seconds later I felt the mental link connect, along with the sensations of three other presences. One was a focused maelstrom—Hasebe, I thought. Nic's gentle strength came through loud and clear, while Finn's crackling determination was a bonfire in through the link.

"Is this what a wireless router feels when it connects to the internet?"

I hadn't meant to project the thought, but Nic's smooth chuckle rolled through my mind.

"It's possible. I've never asked one to know for sure."

"Be alert," Hasebe said, his voice bringing a wave of primal discipline through the link. *"Once we reach the island, our presence will be known. We will have to strike quickly and with brutal force."*

I pulled the antler handle knife from its sheath, holding the flat edge against my forearm. This was it.

CHAPTER NINETEEN

ODIN

THE LOCK, CELTIC SEA

The little island hadn't changed much in eight years. A few of the tall, dead trees were fallen over, and the beach's sand was still the same dark grey-black.

The oppressive aura of magic emanating from the place was new, though. The closer we got, the more I felt a pressure inside my head that threatened to make my eardrums burst.

"Is this how it's supposed to feel?"

"Yeah, no," Finn projected. *"There's supposed to be a little ambient magic around the Lock, it's been that way for a thousand years. Not like this. This is wrong."*

"They have begun," Nic said. He sounded more solemn than usual.

"Are we too late?" I said. *"Has he killed her already?"*

"Hard to say. The currents of magic are certainly aggravated, but not what I'd expect to feel if the Serpent Ritual had truly activated. We may be in time."

"I remember this island providing some sort of geographic awareness of itself," I said. *"Is that still the case?"*

"It will be the case for those of us with magic." Finn grimaced. *"I'm sorry, Hasebe."*

"This is not my world," my bodyguard sent, checking his Cobalt. *"I would have expected no less. I will adapt."*

"Which means Odin and Juno will both be aware of us as soon as we set foot on the island," I said. *"We'll need to move quickly and decisively. Don't give him an opportunity to retreat or strike first."*

Hasebe bared his teeth in a predatory grin. *"Finally."*

He holstered his revolver and snapped a silvery-black machine gun to a strap on the tactical vest he'd put on beneath his sport coat. I brought the catamaran to a stop floating just above the beach. Nic clicked his fingers, dispelling the working with a snap of breaking stone. Sounds rushed back into my ears as we rushed to the side of the 'boat nearest the black sand of the beach.

"Go!"

I vaulted over the side, landing on the sand with a dull thump. Awareness flooded my perception, like returning to an old home. Two electric presences shimmered near the old stone hut on the north side of the island. One had the same thunderstorm power I'd first felt from Snorri back in Johannesburg. The other was a violent monsoon, dangerous yet familiar. Cari.

Alongside them was a discordant mess of energy, a black hole in the magical tension surrounding the island.

The ritual... whatever they've done, it's drawing in power.

I took off in a sprint towards the hut, Finn and Hasebe close behind. Though Hasebe lacked the intrinsic knowledge of the terrain we now had, he kept up well.

We burst into the clearing around the stone hut just to pull up short as a bolt of fire came to meet us. I dodged left, scurrying along the tough grass.

Through the doorway of the dilapidated hut, a tall figure forced its way into the clearing. His size was the same, but something about

Snorri's bearing felt different. The tailored pastel blue suit hung looser on his frame. Added to the malice in his one-eyed glare, the impact was wildly different. The black eyepatch covering his left eye only added to that sense of malice.

"I should have killed you both in Africa," he said, his accent harsher and more guttural than Snorri's had been.

"Your mistake," Hasebe growled. He snapped off a burst of automatic fire.

His shots stopped dead against a sparkling quarter-dome of light that appeared in front of the big man.

"Get Juno!" Finn sent. *"We'll hold him off."*

"Don't die while I'm working."

I took a step towards the hut, only to be nearly crisped by another fiery bolt. It met a glob of water centimetres from my face and exploded in a cloud of steam.

I shot Finn a grateful look. It was all either of us could spare. Raising my left hand, I thrust down at the ground with a bark of, *"Uruz!"*

I'm still not sure if it was the focus ring or the increased magic in the air around me that did it. Either way, instead of launching myself a foot or two into the air, I flew up in a high arc that brought me tumbling down on the far side of the hut. I rolled, bruising both forearms. Still, at least they weren't broken.

"Are you alright?" Finn asked in my head.

"Fine," I sent, the thought as sharp as the pain. *"Focus on not dying."*

I pulled myself to a seated position, back against the stone wall that vibrated with magic. No sign of my best friend yet. I'd have to look elsewhere.

The black hole pulsed against my magical senses, just on the opposite side of the stone wall. I tried to glimpse it in my farsight and almost vomited as the sheer density of magic washed over me.

Stupid... I should have tried to get a peek of the ritual formation while I was hurtling over top of it.

Jumping in there blind seemed a foolhardy idea, especially if Cari were still in there.

"Why are you so determined to ruin everything for me?"

The sound of my best friend's voice made me look up. Cari, wearing a teal blue surcoat over her charcoal grey fatigues, stood off to my left. One hand was curled into a fist. She held a thick leather book in the other.

"Good to see you too," I said, my voice flat. "I haven't been trying to find you for two years or anything."

"I told you not to," she said, hair and irises blazing with blue fire. "I told you to leave me alone."

"And I told you that I was trying to help you, Cari. What has Odin promised you that I couldn't?"

She flinched—not a big motion, but I saw it.

"De la Cruz told you, then," Cari said. "I wondered if he'd survive."

"He survived, all right," I said. "Nic also told me you kept him alive. Kept Odin from killing him."

"The Valdisson is too useful to just slaughter like an animal," Cari said, just a little too quickly.

"Nic does seem to be very good at what he does," I said, reaching out with my farsight toward her—

not now Can't give up now We're so close Just let me do this I need control of my power I'm still too weak My magic is too—

"Stop that!" Cari snarled, holding up a tiny ball of blue fire between two fingers. "I can feel you pushing on my mind. Leave me alone."

"What are you so afraid of, Cari?" I asked, taking a steadying breath. "That's not like you."

From the other side of the stone hut came Hasebe's bellowing battle cry, followed by the stuttering fire of his machine gun.

"You don't know what I've had to do, Brooke. Magic came so easily for you. You knew what to do as soon as you had it. I had to struggle and grasp at whatever straws I could find. Chris was on purpose, but I hurt so many people by accident. Even you. My power fought me every chance it got."

"Because you opened yourself up and just let the pool pour raw magic into you," I said, shaking my head. "There was a whole priming process you skipped. And anyway, you know more about all this mythology than some professors. Surely that counts for something."

"I know enough to be sure that Odin knows what he's talking about. Killing Nidhogg and taking in its power is the only way I can gain true knowledge of my magic. That's the only way I'll ever get full control and stop hurting people."

"Who told you that, Odin?"

The ground shook as a wave of force rippled through it. Several of the nearby trees cracked, exposing naked wood.

"Odin taught me enough to know that learning on my own will be more helpful," Cari said. "He had to make a sacrifice to learn magic. So will I."

I took the opening. "What exactly are you prepared to sacrifice this time? Everything? The little you have left?"

It was hard to read, but I saw hesitation in her glowing eyes.

"Brooke?" Finn said in my head. *"I'm running out of steam and Hasebe's down to his last reload."*

I went for the kill. "Did Odin tell you what *he'd* have to sacrifice for this to work?"

"What?"

"Nic told us this ritual requires a blood sacrifice," I said, a wicked grin spreading across my face. "I'm guessing Odin left that part out. He's playing you, like he's been doing to everyone for God only knows how long."

"No, he..." she trailed off, eyes cooling to an orange shimmer as they clouded with confusion. "He said that wasn't necessary anymore."

Cari's eyes flared blue again. "Stop trying to scare me! Why would you lie to me about that?"

"Why would he? Surely if Odin is helping you learn to control your magic, he'd have told you the correct way to perform the ritual that will get you that knowledge."

"Brooke!" Finn's sending was more urgent this time. *"Help would be great!"*

"Why wouldn't Odin tell you the ritual still needs a sacrifice?" I pressed. "Who do you think he's planning to sacrifice for it, huh? Himself? Or some mouthy girl who's no longer useful to him?"

"I got him the grimoire," Cari snapped. "And the smith! How could he say I'm not useful after all that?"

"He's planning to use you as the sacrifice, Cari," I said. "I can't prove that, I'll admit it up front, but why else would he not have cared about Nic? Why would Odin have left him in Bergen, rather than bringing him with you to come here?"

"He was too useful to kill," she said, a defiant set to her jaw. "The ritual doesn't need a sacrifice anymore."

"Did you read that? Or did he tell you that was the case?" I said, sliding my back up the wall. I was out of time. Hasebe was down, and both he and Finn would likely be dead soon if I didn't return to the fight.

"Where are you going?" she said. "We're not done."

"Read the damn journal, Cari! Odin's plan benefits no one but himself and may even break reality if Nic is right. He wants you dead. You're nothing to him. You never were. I still believe in you. Do the right thing for once in your life."

Without another word, I pushed off and charged around the side of the stone hut. Glowing golden light flared through the tattoos beneath my sleeve as I drew deeply on my magic, readying myself.

I flipped my antler-handled knife, gripping it by the blade. The moment Odin's broad back came into view I hurled my knife at him. It stuck in the centre of his left shoulder blade, causing the big man to roar in pain.

He whirled. I saw the fury in his one golden eye.

"Impudent child!" Odin spat. "Why do you impede my efforts to save the world?"

"Don't come crying to me with your noble intentions, " I snapped. "We both know it's not true."

His suit, now that I had a good look, was spattered with blood all along the left side. Several long gashes marred the expensive fabric. Hasebe had gotten lucky.

"Nidhogg will be of no further threat to me once it is slain!" Odin said, teeth bared as he reached back over his shoulder. "Or anyone else. Even you should be able to see that."

"Possibly, if that was all you wanted," I said, holding up my left hand. "But we both know it isn't."

"What would you know of what I want, little *merr*?" Odin snarled. "You are as dull as that mutt who follows you around everywhere. You know nothing of the world, or of magic. My father created the magic you toss about so carelessly!"

"I don't care if you do think yourself a god," I said, rage bubbling over. "Your utter disdain for everyone who isn't you is deplorable. I won't let you kill my best friend just to make yourself more powerful. *Laguz!*"

I lashed out at Odin with a burst of water, aiming for his chest. It missed as he dodged backward, striking him full in the face instead. The big man spluttered, whatever rune he'd been about to say interrupted. I took advantage of the brief respite to glance around our battlefield.

Hasebe knelt at the edge of the clearing, machine gun on the ground beside him. He was sliding rounds into his Cobalt, mouth twisted in an impatient snarl.

"Brooke!" Finn's voice came from my left. I spun, catching sight of him kneeling on the ground. He threw out a hand, pointing behind me. "Knife!"

The warning came almost too late. I threw myself to the side, feeling the red-hot flash of pain as my knife sliced through the top of my shoulder.

I yelped, using a burst of force magic to toss myself further in that direction. I got out of the way but only just. Drawing up water, I hurled it at Odin. I hit him in the face again, making him stumble a step.

"Uruz!" I snapped, stomping on the ground as I unleashed a directed shock of force magic through it. Odin sidestepped my attack, darting forward with one hand outstretched.

"Juno has more raw power, but you'll do for a sacrifice," he growled, clamping his hand around my right forearm so hard both bones snapped. That tore a scream from me, blanketing my brain in agony. It was all I could do to stay conscious.

"Isa!" someone shouted.

I was weightless for an eternity before my head bounced off the rough ground. The pain jolted some part of my poor brain back to awareness, enough to see Odin stagger again, his right arm covered in frost. I pushed myself up as best I could on my good arm. Without another thought I drew deeply on the scraps of my power, lashing out with a shout of, *"Uruz!"*

A wave of invisible force ploughed a line of earth in its wake as it smashed into Odin's chest, sending the big man falling to the ground on his backside. The battlefield fell silent for a moment, as Odin and I made stunned eye contact with one another. Neither of us had expected my attack to hit quite that hard.

Odin recovered first. The big man roared, smashing a fist into the ground. Much as before, a ripple of invisible force pulsed through the ground, tearing large chunks of it free. It wouldn't have taken much to make me fall again, and that was more than enough. I hit the ground again on my face, the bone-deep ache in my arm making it hard to think. Chunks of soil tumbled over me, half-burying me in the aftermath of Odin's attack.

"You are wasting my time, foolish child," Odin said. Bastard didn't even sound winded. "The foundations have been laid for hours. My window is closing rapidly to summon the dragon."

I was yanked out of the dirt and thrown to the ground. A foot came down hard on my back, forcing the air from my lungs in a pained wheeze.

"These fools are a far cry from my Aesir, my valkyries," he continued. His voice sounded wistful, unless that was my oxygen-deprived imagination. "Juno is the closest I have seen in centuries, yet even she is a pale imitation. You will suffice in her stead."

The foot pressed down harder, putting pressure on my spine. An odd sensation stirred the currents of magic around me, as though someone had taken a deep breath. A harsh male voice began chanting. This time I didn't recognize the words.

With a snap of power, I felt a magic circle close around me. Forcing my head up, I found myself lying on the ground in a ritual circle, Odin kneeling before me. He held my knife clutched in his right hand. With the fingers of his other hand he marked the ground with runes whose power radiated a biting cold. His motions were quick and precise, just as Nic's had been. The black hole of magic moved, hovering just above me now.

Odin reached up, a six-pronged crystalline antler materialising in his hand.

That... whatever that is, it's the source of the black hole. The ritual working.

Holding the knife in his other hand like a quill, Odin touched its tip to my cheek and made two delicate cuts in the shape of two right angles whose arms almost touched.

Jera, I thought with what was left of my fading strength. *The symbol of crossing a threshold. What a perfect sacrificial mark.*

Hot, sticky blood flowed down my cheek, making a pool under my face. The smell of copper filled my nose. I should have tried to fight, to escape and push back. Instead my body rebelled, exhausted from shock and fatigue. Even my magic had failed me. My mind was too foggy. I couldn't remember the rune words, never mind what they did. It was only through my gift of knowledge I'd even picked up on how Odin had marked me, futile though it was.

Something flared white at the edge of my vision, along with the whuff of extinguishing flame. Behind Odin, I thought I made out a cluster of falling sparks. Someone had thrown a fire bolt at the invisible shield made by Odin's ritual circle. That was futile, too. Magic couldn't get in or out of a circle once it had fully closed.

Two voices, blurred and distorted by the concentrated field of magic, shouted back and forth. I couldn't make out the words.

Odin's scarred fingers came into view as he dipped them into the shallow pool of my blood. He smeared some of it across my forehead, then across the blade of my knife.

"Behold, Nidhogg, end-bringer," he said, speaking several languages all at once. *"Here is a sacrifice of blood for your passage."*

I closed my eyes, wanting to meet my death with as much decorum as I had left.

It was all that saved my vision.

A shot rang out, followed by the sound of breaking glass. Mottled red-white light flared its assault against my closed eyelids.

Odin screamed.

CHAPTER TWENTY

DAUGHTERS OF THE AESIR

I opened my eyes to find the world around me on fire.

A wall of blue-orange flames four or five feet high formed a giant circle around the clearing, scorching the earth down to bare soil. Only the stone hut and the motionless bodies littered around the clearing were not on fire. The heat was not as intense as it should have been for flames of that size, though I still found myself sweating.

Odin lay slumped on the ground in front of me, almost mirroring my pose. Ragged cloth surrounded a gaping hole in his shoulder. There was no sign of the crystalline antler, nor the oppressive tension of the congealed ritual magic.

Cari, aiming Hasebe's Cobalt revolver at the big man, stood over the two of us.

"Liar."

She pulled the trigger again.

The report was deafening as the gun bucked in her hands. Odin screamed again as her shot went through the back of his right calf in an explosion of blood and bits.

A hand fell on my back. I twisted my head in that direction to find Finn's grimy face staring down at me.

"Are you dead?" he asked as he knelt beside me. His irises were golden now, a sign he was holding his magic close to the surface.

"No," I managed. "But only just."

"Do you have enough juju left to patch yourself up?"

Oh. I could do that, I suppose.

Reaching to my magic again, I slurred out, *"Sowilo."*

A tingle of energy rushed through my battered body, closing the wound on my cheek. I knew from prior experimentation it would take more than I could manage at present to heal my broken bones. At least this way I wasn't on the verge of collapsing from shock anymore. I shuddered, pushing myself onto my back with my good arm.

In front of us, Cari lashed out with a booted foot, kicking Odin in the back of the head.

"Think you can just use me and throw me away? I read le Fay's grimoire. I know what you intended. I'm not your damn fetch-dog, you—"

Odin's hand shot back, gripping the Cobalt by its barrel. With a deft motion, he yanked it free of Cari's grasp and clubbed her across the face with a crack of bone. He struck out with his good leg, sending Cari off balance to the ground.

"Know your place, *seidhkona*," he spat, rising to his feet. He growled, favouring his injured leg. "Had I still Gungnir in my possession, you would be dead."

Cari locked both hands around his ankle. *"Burn like Muspell, deceiver."*

Blue flames engulfed Odin's calf, surging up his leg and one side of his body. He jerked backward, dropping the gun as he slapped at his ragged suit with his good hand. The big man stumbled and fell backwards, landing hard on the scorched ground.

Cari rose like a vengeful angel, wiping blood from her face. He'd broken her nose, from the look of it.

Finn helped me to my knees, a look of stunned awe on his face as he glanced up and saw the flaming circle.

"Bloody hell," he whispered. "I didn't know you could make a circle that big."

"Neither did she," I said, coughing. "Come on. We have to finish this."

Odin thrust a hand into the air and called, *"Huginn! Muninn! To me!"*

Two dark shapes detached from a treetop outside the circle of fire, cawing loud enough to be heard over the roar of the flames. Light flashed as the two birds pecked at the fiery wall of magical energy we stood inside.

"Your birds won't help you here," Cari said, her broken nose imparting an odd, nasal tone. "I ought to stitch your lying mouth shut, as was done to Loki in the stories. You don't care about me at all."

Odin glared up at her. "Short-sighted fool. Ragnarök will be the end of everything, not just you! Loki's vermin must not be allowed to survive if I am to live and continue to share my knowledge."

"People thought 2012 would be the end of the world too," Cari said, sniffling as she wiped more blood from her face. "Yet here we are anyway. I think you lied about that too "

"Power is a fantastic motivator to lie," I said, wincing as Finn helped me stand. "I've seen that one personally."

"Shut up, Brooke," Cari said. "This is between me and the old man."

She spit off to one side, turning back to Odin. "I should have known better than to trust you."

"You should also have known better than to give me time to recover my strength."

Odin shot to his feet, moving almost faster than I could see, and headbutted Cari square in the face. Doubled over like that, he slammed the ground with his good hand again and snarled, *"Hagalaz!"*

As if empowered by his words, the two birds both broke through the wall of magic at the same time, shattering it with their beaks as Odin's hex weakened the circle from the inside. The circle of flames died out, extinguished by a rush of wind and wings. Huginn and Muninn dived towards Odin, the former reaching him first.

"We need to get out of here," Finn said in my ear. "He's going to kill all of us if we don't."

"I don't want Cari anywhere near Nic," I said back. "And we can barely move ourselves, let alone Hasebe."

That thought finally connected in my battered head—I hadn't seen Hasebe in a fair while. With it came a sick feeling in my stomach. If he wasn't here... there was likely only one reason.

Bile rose in my throat as I realised Odin would probably get away with having ended Hasebe's life. He'd been a good bodyguard and a better advisor for so long.

It can't end like this... but what else can I do?

The big man rose to his full height, towering over Cari with the two large birds perched on his shoulders.

"When I am done with you, *merr*, you will wish I had killed you here," he growled.

"Then face me, *argr*," Cari shot back, clenching her left fist. "Unless you really are as cowardly as the giants said you were."

My gift didn't translate the insults the two were exchanging. It only seemed to care about Old Norse words that were directly related to magic or the runes I wielded. But whatever Cari had called him was far worse.

Odin staggered back a step like she'd slapped him across the face. He pounded a fist to his chest, bellowing a war cry as his two ravens joined in.

"You take that back!" he roared, charging at Cari. Odin bodied her to the ground, sending the much smaller woman tumbling back several feet. In reply, she loosed a bolt of fire at him that almost took out the raven on his right shoulder. Cari rolled, coming up into a crouch from which she tossed several more firebolts at Odin.

A pang of envy flashed through my chest. Just how deep were her reserves of magic? She'd called on it much more than I had even in this single fight and didn't look remotely winded from it, save her bloody nose.

Odin dodged the first two attacks, catching the third across his broad forearm. Flames chewed away at his sleeve, but he hardly seemed to notice this time. Instead, the big man spat a word and his ravens took to the air. Two more of him shimmered into existence, one on either side where the ravens had been.

Cari snarled, "A hall of mirrors won't save you from me, oath-breaker! You're dead."

She clenched her fist, then flung her hand toward Odin.

"Kenaz!"

The ground tore open, gouts of fire exploding upward to engulf the two illusory Odins. The big man swore, his ravens cawing at Cari as they took to the air again, circling their master's head.

I stood in awe, enraptured by the sheer display of magical power at play. Could I come anywhere close to this someday, if I were to get some proper training?

Finn tugged on my arm, breaking the reverie. "Let's go. This is what we wanted, right? Our ace up the sleeve?"

"Not without Hasebe. I don't care if he's dead. He deserves better than to be left here to rot."

The blue-haired man hauled me back a few feet as Odin deflected another of Cari's firebolts into the scorched ground, almost catching my boots in the splatter of magical fire.

"She can't beat him! There's no way. Listen, Brooke, I know she's your friend but he's a bleedin' bedtime story."

As if she'd heard him, Cari spread her arms wide, elbows bent and fist clenched. She gave a war cry much like Odin had, but instead of charging, she reached to her waist and yanked loose a thin length of silvery, sparkling cord. Power rolled off it in waves, its aura almost visible.

Cari flicked her wrist, sending the cord whipping around Odin's neck once, then twice. The other end dangled loose, almost to his ribcage.

It was only when she charged forward and grasped both ends that I realised what she was holding.

Finn beat me to it, letting out a curse under his breath. "Gleipnir."

"Nic's unbreakable, impossible creation," I said. "It's beautiful."

"I take it back. She might actually kill him with that. Holy hell."

Cari screamed again, digging her heels and pulling back as if holding the reins of a stubborn horse. Odin jerked backward against the thread, his eye bulging wide and desperate. The ravens leapt free and began circling Cari, pecking at her forearms and face.

"Die, you bastard!" she screamed, her words laced with fire. Both ravens fluttered out of the way of Cari's dragon breath.

I stood slumped against Finn as we watched, frozen again in horrified fascination. Even in my strangest nightmares I never thought I'd see an ancient god garrotted by a piece of fairy-tale magic. This whole mess was becoming more and more ludicrous by the minute.

A far more realistic sound cut through Odin's choking gargles—the chatter of automatic gunfire.

One of the circling ravens exploded in a burst of feathers. Several shots tore through Odin's right arm as they passed by Cari on that side. She ducked, letting go of Gleipnir with one hand. That gave Odin just enough of an opening to wrench himself free from the cord, blood dribbling from thin slices in his neck. He fell to one knee, fingers scrabbling in the dirt as he traced out several runes.

Drawing on my power one last time, I lashed out with invisible force.

"Uruz!"

The force burst I'd conjured smashed him full in the chest, knocking him to the sooty dirt on his back. Before I or anyone else could stop him, Odin slammed his hand on the runes he'd drawn and gasped out, *"Raidho!"*

A cold, twisting sensation filled the air, accompanied by the ubiquitous electric tang of magic. Odin's tortured body blurred, then faded from sight. The still-living raven vanished the same way, though not before fixing me with the most soul-searching gaze I'd ever seen from an animal. Both were gone within seconds, leaving nothing but blood and feathers behind.

Cari dropped to her knees, chest heaving beneath her combat blouse. She wasn't holding the Cobalt. Nor had Odin been, for that matter. So where had those shots come from?

My heart surged as Hasebe, one eye blackened and his suit torn and bloody, staggered into the scorched clearing.

It plummeted as he trained his automatic rifle on Cari's exposed back and growled, "You are not long for this world, Juno."

Before I could stop him, Hasebe fired a chattering burst from his rifle.

CHAPTER TWENTY-ONE

ASHES

If he'd taken the time to aim, Cari would have died then and there. Fortunately for my best friend and Hasebe his shots went wide, only one grazing her forearm.

"Damn you, stop shooting me!" Cari said, gritting her teeth as she spun to face him, clamping one hand around her new injury. "I still have scars from the last time."

I let go of Finn's shoulder and held up my good hand. "Wait, Hasebe!"

He swore in Japanese. "Even now, you hesitate?"

"I hesitate when she may be able to tell us something about our true adversary," I snapped, too exhausted to be diplomatic. "Know your place, Yorimoto."

"I'm out of magic anyway," Cari said, her voice shaky. "Sorta surprised I'm still conscious, actually."

Hasebe's eyes went cold, but he lowered the rifle to point at Cari's toes rather than her heart.

"There is wisdom in what my employer suggests," he said. "Speak, Juno. What is your intent, now that Odin has departed?"

Cari sniffled, wiping at her face with a hand. Her lower face and chin were covered in blood from her nose, like a macabre half-mask.

"I have no idea where he's gone, before you ask," she said. Blue flames danced in her eyes, but that was as far as it went. Her hair had returned to its normal coffee brown. "Clearly I don't know him as well as he made me think I did."

"You didn't visit any of his safe houses, his secret forges?" Finn asked. "We found the one in Bergen."

"What kind of idiot are you?" Cari said, wiping her face with a sleeve. "I didn't even know we were going to Norway until he told me to take de la Cruz there. The man trusts nobody with nothing."

"He trusted you to steal le Fay's journal," I said.

"And then tried to kill me with it. Good thing he was stupid enough to keep the book and the cipher in the hut, at least. He can't try the Serpent Ritual again without that grimoire."

"This does not answer my question," Hasebe said, raising his rifle again.

"Then let me finish," Cari said, glaring at him. "I'll give you the blasted grimoire, it's of no use to me. Even with le Fay's cipher the thing is on a level I can barely understand. All I want in exchange for the books is to be left alone."

"Sorry, but no," Finn said.

Cari and I both turned to stare at him. Alarm swelled in my heart. Had I misjudged Finn? Here at the last, was he going to stick to rules and protocols after all?

"We have a bigger problem to deal with," he continued. "Odin has infiltrated the White Order. We have no idea how long he's been there or what he plans on doing, but it's likely he knows a great deal more than Lía would be comfortable with. Not to mention the people he may have turned to his side while he was there."

Finn's face lost all expression, another diplomatic tell I recognised. "And if the Serpent Ritual is any indication, he's more than willing to destroy the mortal world to achieve his goal of prolonging his life."

His words hung in the air for a long moment. Hasebe was the first to break the silence.

"Hm. The enemy of our enemy. Is this what you propose?"

Cari snorted, followed by a curse and a hand to her nose. "If you're proposing we team up so you can help me kill Odin, I'm okay with that. I owe him some payback for trying to off both of us."

Hasebe made a low noise in his throat. It wasn't quite a growl. "As do I. That is the last time I will let him call me a dog."

"How in the bloody hell are we going to kill Odin?" I said, feeling the tension in my shoulders go up another notch. My broken arm was aching again. "He took all four of us down almost without effort."

"I haven't got that far yet," Finn said. "But we need to tell Lía, if no one else."

"If you think she'll listen," I said. The Keepers in Bergen had said both Morgana and Snorri sent them after us. If that was the case, our odds were terrible.

"She'll listen to me."

His voice was hard and determined, making me take a step back.

"Either way, I'll need more training," I said, glancing between Finn and Cari. "The ring helps, but not if I don't know how to evocate properly. There's still so much about magic I don't know."

"Don't look at me," Cari said. "I got my magic the wrong way, remember? I can do a lot of things, but teaching is not one of them."

"Says the one who's got a pair of doctorates," I said, cracking a smile.

"Cari Edwards does," she said, but there was a mischievous glint in her eye. "I don't."

"Physical training will be difficult," Hasebe said. "I will leave the *yokai* business to Aalto-san."

"Have fun with that," Cari said, dusting off her surcoat. "In the meantime, I have some stuff to take care of."

"We're not done—" Finn started, but she cut him off.

"I'll be in touch, Bluey, don't worry. At least, while we have a common enemy."

"How did you two get here?" I asked. "We had a 'boat."

"I teleported, obviously." Cari shook her head. "Bastard finally clued me in on how Bridges work, just in time to try and kill me for knowing too much."

"It's not teleporting," Finn said. "It just looks like—oh, forget it. Too complex to explain here."

"Whatever, it was a joke. After the Bridge to Bristol, we came here on an old-school 'boat from a different side of the island than you and I crashed on."

I nodded. "It's still there. Pieces of the 'boat, I mean."

"I noticed." Cari shuddered. "I'm sort of surprised, actually. I thought the namby-pamby wizards would've gotten rid of all the technology on their precious island."

"Stones of David, we're not the bloody Amish!" Finn said, throwing his hands up. "Modern technology just doesn't coexist well with magic. It takes a while for the magic to reacclimate."

"Does it, now?" Cari's eyes sparkled with familiar curiosity. "That would explain a lot."

Hasebe sighed. "This place is compromised. If we're going to talk, let us at least go back to the hoverboat. All the medical supplies are there."

Cari shook her head. "I'm getting out of here. Back to one of my little hidey-holes to lick my wounds and plan my vengeance."

I sighed. "Right, it worked so well the last time."

"Whatever doesn't kill me," she said, limping off towards the forest. Halfway across the scorched clearing, she stopped and turned back to face me. "I'll contact you when I know anything. Has your phone number changed?"

"Not in the last couple years," I said. Bitter warmth welled up in my chest. She'd kept my phone number, despite vanishing into nowhere for two years.

"Good. I'll be in touch."

She turned and disappeared into the trees.

"At least you survived," I said under my breath. "There may still be hope for you, Cari."

⋖∏⋙

Nic looked as worried as I'd ever seen him when we returned to the catamaran.

"When I saw the circle of flames, I thought that was the end for you, little raven," he said as Finn put my arm in a splint. "That sort of magic circle never spells good things."

By some miracle, even though we'd all sustained cuts and bruises from nearly being beaten to a stain, I was the only one who'd broken a bone. I hadn't even been fighting when it occurred.

I nodded, trying to keep the discomfort off my face. "It was a near thing. Turns out Odin never expected to get shot in the leg by his dupe."

Nic sucked in a breath. "You mean Juno is still alive?"

"We seem to have a truce," I said. "As long as Odin remains alive, that is. She means to slay him."

Nic blinked. "Well. She's crazy after all, it seems."

"We're thinking along similar lines."

"As are you, in that case," Nic said. He turned toward Finn. "Does she still have the le Fay books?"

"I've got them," Finn said. "They're staying with me for the time being. Even when we go back to Gladsheim."

"Can we tell the White Order anything at this point?" I said. "You said yourself we don't know who may or may not be under Odin's influence."

"No, I don't. But I also know what the Keepers will try and do to you if I don't bring you back to Reykjavik. I'm going to be in enough trouble for what happened in Bergen. That's blown any shreds of plausible deniability I might've had out the window."

"Now wait just a moment," I said, twisting away from Finn. I regretted it an instant later as pain shot up my arm. "Damn it all!"

"Hold still, then," Finn said, taking my arm between his hands again. He began to wrap thin metal mesh around the broken section ."I'm not forcing you to join up with the Order. That's your decision. Just know that if I get my way they'll try to recruit you, if only to keep you quiet. "

"I've kept secrets my whole life. One more won't do much."

I gritted my teeth as Finn finished the splint. Once done, he tapped the mesh he'd wrapped my arm in with a small galvaniser rod. The electromagnetic tourniquet mesh tightened in an instant, holding my arm in place. I relaxed a little.

When he was finished, Finn dusted his hands together and rose, extending his arms over his head. He winced. "Probably a bit too soon for stretching the ribs. I don't have any affinity for the healing rune. You'll be right as rain in a month or two, on the other hand."

"It's never worked that fast before," I said, flexing my fingers as best I could. "The Sowilo rune can't heal such major injuries, and my herbal poultices can only do so much."

"Even using the rune on your injuries every day?"

I kept my face neutral, but inside I let out a swear.

Using the healing rune on a daily basis had never occurred to me. It was a bloody good idea, too. I'd assumed for years the speed of my body's natural healing process could only be sparked off by use of the Sowilo rune, and only once per wound If the reality was that I could use the rune daily, well...

"I've never tried," I admitted.

Nic chuckled, turning it into a cough as I shot him a frosty glare.

Hasebe met my eye, then flicked his gaze belowdecks, to the captain's stateroom. His leg and arms were bandaged. I hadn't seen him do that, but it couldn't have been the others. Hasebe wouldn't have asked them to.

I got to my feet, only wavering a little.

"Beg your pardon," I said. "I need to check on something belowdecks. There should be a fully-stocked chiller cabinet under one of the bench seats."

"I'd settle for a Guinness, but I doubt you have any," Finn said, his accent thickening.

I rolled my eyes. "Amuse yourselves and don't break my 'boat. I'll return shortly."

One hand on the railing, I descended to the stateroom. Hasebe followed me in, closing the door behind him. I sank down on the thin mattress, staring up at Hasebe. He'd stripped off his burnt and bloodied suit jacket, leaving him in his stained shirt sleeves.

"I forgot myself in Norway," he said in Japanese, crossing arms over his chest. "But I can contain myself no longer."

Hasebe took a long breath through his nose. "Have you lost your mind?"

I almost laughed. It was the wrong response, but I was all sorts of scrambled after that level of fighting. "Hasebe, I know I've asked a lot of you the past week or so, but—"

"That is not what I'm talking about. Why did you let Carissa live? *Again?*"

His tone didn't change, but I could see the anger in my bodyguard's eyes.

"Her *yokai* gifts are strong, that cannot be denied," he said. "She will be an asset against Odin. But I fear for your safety knowing that she still lives. It seems foolish to trust her like this, having only her word that she will aid us. When you have to shoot, shoot. Don't talk."

I swallowed, my mouth and throat parched. Quotes aside, he was right. I'd nearly gotten Hasebe killed a dozen times over during this whole mess. I'd thought he had died at the Lock. I needed to give him something, a shred of whatever reassurance I could muster.

I took a deep breath through my nose, replying in Japanese on the exhale.

"Finn was teasing me earlier about sensing good in Cari. It may be a touch pedantic, but he's right. There's a little part of me that just doesn't want to give up on her.

"However," I added, sensing a rebuttal coming, "there's a more pragmatic reason. Did you see what she did to Odin on the island?"

"I did not," Hasebe admitted. "I was knocked senseless and only recovered in time to see her standing before you again."

"She went toe-to-toe with Odin—and almost killed him. Granted, it was due to a sneaky trick, garotting him with that unbreakable cord, but even you must admit that's better than you fared against him."

The muscles in his jaw bunched, but Hasebe gave a small nod. "He is a formidable enemy. I've never encountered anything like him before."

I winced. That admission had cost him no small amount of pride.

"I'm sorry," I said. "But that proves my point. We cannot trust the wizards, they've been standoffish and held out on us at every turn. Not to mention any of them might be influenced by Snorri. Finn and Nic seem to be the sole exceptions. That makes them alone our allies in this. You saw how badly the four of us fared against Odin. We have no choice, Hasebe."

Hasebe's eyes softened, even if his bearing didn't.

I pressed on. "Cari is too powerful a force to ignore when we have no other allies to reasonably turn to. What would your contacts say if you told them you needed their aid in slaying someone thought to be a myth, a bedtime story?"

I leaned forward, resting my forearms on my thighs. "By stopping his scheme, I became a threat to Odin. We all did. He knows we want him dead. If we don't strike him down first, he will find us. And he will kill us. Unless we take every ally, every trick, every possible aid we can get. There are two kinds of people in the world, Yorimoto. Those with loaded guns—"

"—and those who dig," Hasebe said, finishing the quote. He stroked his short beard, his gaze drifting to the ceiling. Neither of us spoke, the silence stretching out to an awkward length.

My bodyguard's shoulders slumped, and he let out a sigh. "From the first time we met, you have made my job complicated. I will not pretend to fully understand this *yokai* business, but it seems we have long passed the point of returning. We must be the ones with loaded guns. But know that while you offer your hand in friendship towards Juno, my hands are armed beside you."

Under the circumstances, it was the best I could've hoped from Hasebe.

I nodded my approval. "Thank you, Yorimoto. Your support means a great deal."

"Do not make me regret this. If another principal dies on my watch, I will never recover from the shame."

"Then let's make sure Odin dies first," I said, sounding far more confident than I felt. I got to my feet as Hasebe opened the door. Together, we returned to the top deck where Finn and Nic were sitting. Neither had helped themselves to any of the beverages on offer, it seemed.

"...I forget how much there is to know sometimes," Nic was saying. "I'm sixteen years older than Morgana, after all. I've learned a great deal in my time."

"Are there any of you *yokai* younger than a century?" Hasebe asked, shaking his head.

"A dozen or so," Nic said, rocking a flat palm side-to-side. "You're standing next to the youngest master wizard since 1970, though."

Finn coughed, a touch of pink peeking through the grime on his cheeks.

"And you?" Hasebe said.

"Appointed master in 1901, if you must know," Nic said, scratching his cheek. "Emigrated to San Diego after finishing my Valdisson apprenticeship in Venice."

"Gentlemen," I said in my aristocratic voice, "we're getting off subject. Have we made any headway on the Odin problem?"

"Right, Odin," Nic said. "I have no idea what we're going to do about him. It's going to be a mess no matter what."

"Worst-case scenario: what happens if we return to Reykjavik and inform the Althing and Morgana about Odin?"

Finn tapped the lounge ceiling with two fingers. "We don't even get to the Althing because 'Snorri' has barred our way. The Keepers detain you and Hasebe, use the greyer magicks to make you forget everything, and probably strip you of your magic just to be certain you won't ever be a danger."

"Can they do that?" Hasebe said. "I thought stealing magic from another *yokai* was impossible. That was why Odin needed the dragon."

"There are plenty of ways to suppress your memory of it to the point that it atrophies and dies out," Nic said. "It's a very nasty form of illusion magic. If you forget you ever knew anything about magic, you end up forgetting the magic itself. Not pretty, and it takes a long time."

"Second worst-case," Finn said. "We tell someone Odin has influence over, who tells no one but the one man we don't want to know."

"Not a grand start," I said. "What about best-case?"

"The Keepers and Morgana take you seriously, offer some sort of accelerated battle-mage training, and give you the option to join up instead of forcing you."

"That's asking an awful lot of them," I said.

Finn pursed his lips. "Brooke, listen—the four of us don't have the firepower to take on Odin. You saw what just happened. Juno aside, we need resources and any angle we can get here."

"I'm aware of that," I said, glancing at Hasebe. "I also know that your people don't trust me. I'm not keen to blindly pledge myself to a group intent on treating me as a useful asset rather than a person, even if they do decide to go the route of conscription rather than oblivion."

"Lía will listen to me. I can't promise what she'll do, but I know she'll listen."

"What makes you so certain?" Hasebe asked.

Finn flicked his wrist. A playing card appeared in that same hand, emblazoned on one side with a skull made into the ace of spades. No magic there, just stage tricks.

"Seven years I've had this up my sleeve. It's the one thing Lía guaranteed she'd hear me out on."

Wait... is that the ace he mentioned in London?

I'd thought he was being metaphorical at the time, but there it was. Given all the theatrics, I doubted he'd give a straight answer about the card if I asked.

"Fine," I said. "If you're so bloody sure, let's patch ourselves up and go back to Reykjavik. Seems all roads lead there anyway."

CHAPTER TWENTY-TWO

THE ACE IN HIS HEAD

CASTLE GLADSHEIM, REYKJAVIK

"I haven't been to Gladsheim in nearly forty years," Nic said as we entered the castle's vaulted atrium once again. "Still looks the same."

Finn snorted. "I doubt anything's changed."

"That's far enough, Councillor Aalto!"

A group of Keepers, flintlocks drawn, strode toward us. To my chagrin, the one at their head was the same one we'd tangled with in Bergen. Linen bandages were wrapped around his neck, evidence of Hasebe's handiwork. His jaw clenched as he approached.

"No tricks this time, you two. Hands up and step away from the Valdisson."

Nic sighed. Hasebe and I raised our hands, crossing them behind our heads.

We must look a fright, all bruised and bloodied... Perhaps I should've had Westaway stop in Knightsbridge for a change of clothes.

I rolled my eyes. Now was not the time to be concerned with fashion. Time was critical.

Evidently Finn agreed.

"Morgana," he said. "We need to see her. Now."

"She's indisposed. What makes you think—"

"The only person any of you need to see is Keymaster MacCauley," said a voice with an Irish accent. Footsteps clacked on the stairs as Murphy, the smartly-dressed councillor from days earlier, descended. The young guard Gladstone followed close behind him, flanked by a second contingent of Keepers.

Finn sighed. "Hello, John. Glad to see you so concerned about my well-being."

"What I'm concerned about is the safety and security of the wizards here," Murphy said, adjusting his glasses. "Something you seem to care very little about lately. Have you lost your mind?"

"We have a bigger problem than Juno," Finn said, his expression fierce. "Bigger than these two for sure."

"You don't get to be the judge of that!" Gladstone snapped, thrusting out a hand toward me. "You are a traitor to the Order, not to mention aiding two known—"

"*Apprentice Gladstone,*" Finn said, his eyes blazing gold. Currents of magic stirred around him like the undertow of a tsunami. "*I have critical information Morgana must know immediately. Shut up and stand aside. You too, John.*"

Gladstone flinched back, almost catching a foot on the bottom stair.

Standing only inches from Finn, I had to resist the impulse to take a step away. It wasn't a Suggestion, but he'd infused his voice with magic enough to give his voice an almost physical presence as it boomed through the atrium.

See, that's the sort of authority I can respect in a man. Kinda hot, too.

I half-heartedly shoved that thought away again.

"Fine," Murphy said after an awkward silence. He motioned to the other group of Keepers. "Escort them to Morgana's private study. If they try anything, kill them. Morgana might decide to do that anyway."

All eighteen Keepers flowed around us, boxing us in.

"My, maybe things have changed," Nic murmured.

The lead Keeper from Bergen offered a shoulder to Nic, but the rest kept their flintlocks raised as we ascended the stairs. I followed close behind Finn, letting Hasebe watch my back.

Several minutes later, the Keepers paused and gestured us through yet another door, this one of dark mahogany.

We emerged from the dim stone hallways into a well-tended garden. Rows of neat flowers sat in raised boxes near the centre of the room. I recognised several of the herbs I used in my healing poultices scattered throughout. This wasn't an ordinary garden, then.

The wall opposite us was lined with books, to my utter lack of surprise. It had been a running theme for every wizard's personal workspace I'd seen.

What differed here was the low table, cushions spread on all four sides, that sat in front of the shelves. A steaming pot rested on a tray in the centre of the table, surrounded by all the appropriate bits and bobs for tea.

Morgana, dressed in an earth-stained tan jinbei, sat on one of the cushions. She had been holding a cup of tea but now set it down on a saucer, turning as the Keepers flowed in behind us.

"Councillor Aalto requested—" the Keeper from Bergen started.

"Why has Valdisson de la Cruz not received medical care, Keeper Jurgen?"

His eyes widened. "I-I was simply following Councillor Murphy's instructions."

"Take him to the infirmary for proper assessment and treatment of his injuries." Morgana's gaze fell on Finn. "The rest of you, wait outside. I wish to speak with my apprentice and these two renegades."

Jurgen and the Keepers exchanged concerned glances, but eventually filed out of the room with Nic in tow. Finn approached the table, Hasebe and I following again.

"Explain," Morgana said, her mismatched eyes icy and dangerous. Even that single word shimmered with power.

Finn stopped short, shoving his hands in the pockets of his dark fatigue pants. "Things have been moving quickly since San Diego. I haven't had the opportunity to—"

"You know what I mean, Finn. Not only did you assault a team of Keepers I personally sent to investigate in Norway, you're knowingly aiding and assisting a potential witch who's ignored an explicit instruction to turn herself in. Snorri was convinced she'd bewitched you."

"Odin is kicking around the world again, Lía."

Morgana's expression turned sceptical. "Odin? He hasn't been seen since the Second World War."

"He nearly killed all four of us at the Lock," I said, gesturing to our various injuries. "I think that should—"

"I think the last thing Councillor Aalto told me was that he was departing San Diego in search of Valdisson Nicolás de la Cruz." Morgana's Irish lilt was harsh, much more so than before. "That was days ago and I've heard nothing since. Not even a telegram to say he was going incommunicado."

"Odin attempted to perform the Serpent Ritual from le Fay's grimoire at the Lock," Finn said, sliding the two books across the table towards her. "He conned Juno into doing all his dirty work, getting it set up and stealing the pieces, fully intending to use her as the sacrifice for the ritual."

"And failing Juno, I was the secondary sacrifice," I said, pointing at my cheek.

"So you've read the grimoire," Morgana said.

"Nic told us about it," Finn said. "Apparently this ritual is old Valdisson legend, along with the Open Chain."

"If you truly fought Odin to stop him from summoning Nidhogg, why aren't you all dead? What became of Juno?"

"I was able to prove to Juno that Odin was manipulating her and planned to kill her," I said. "She unleashed her magic and was close to slaying him until he managed to run away. One of his ravens is dead, too."

"That seems exceptionally unlikely, Miss Gilkeson," Morgana said. "Regardless of your nature as Third of this cycle, Juno has evaded the Keepers for over a year and kept a low enough profile that we still don't know anything about her appearance. To be frank, this seems like a desperate attempt to get on my good side. From both of you."

Finn flipped the ace of spades card from his sleeve, slamming it down hard enough to rattle the teapot.

"Lía. It's her."

Morgana stared at the card. Her gaze shifted first to Finn, then to me.

"After all this time?" she said. "You're certain?"

"Card. On table." Finn tapped the playing card.

Silence settled over the table. After what felt like an age and a half, Morgana spoke.

"The rest of you'd better sit down. I've just made some ginseng kapha tea, if you like."

I put up my neutral diplomat's face again. Despite his posturing and theatrics, I hadn't honestly expected Finn's playing card to win him any favour with Morgana.

These people make no bloody sense.

We seated ourselves on the cushions around Morgana's table, the process slow and sore. Hasebe knelt on his cushion, resting both hands on his thighs. His cybernetic hand had been scratched and charred in a few places.

"Is Juno still a threat?" Morgana asked, taking a sip of tea.

"Juno is beside the point," Hasebe said. "Odin has infiltrated your Order, masquerading as Snorri Sturluson."

Her face froze for a heartbeat before the neutral mask slipped into place. The lapse was slight, but I knew what to look for.

"Stones of David," Morgana said, setting her teacup down. "Snorri's come and gone from Gladsheim since I was an apprentice. He was practically a fixture, even before I was elected."

"You see why I was in such a rush to speak with you," Finn said. "We have no idea who might be under Odin's influence. Juno wants to kill him as revenge for trying to sacrifice her in the Serpent Ritual. The three of us and Nic are of a mind to assist."

Her eyes hardened, calculating and assessing, before she turned back to Finn. "And then?"

"We haven't gotten quite that far," I said. "But if any of the legends and folklore about Odin are true, it's going to be a monumental undertaking to slay him. Juno is a secondary concern at this point."

The table went silent, Morgana nodding to herself as she sipped her tea. It gave me more than enough time to worry that we were too late, that Snorri had slid his hooks into her already.

"Councillor Aalto," Morgana said, placing her teacup on its saucer. "This is too grave a matter to assume you're lying to me. Nevertheless, there must be some sort of repercussions for your misbehaviour this past week. As such, I hereby strip you of your rank as Councillor of the High Althing. You will no longer be privy to any of its meetings, nor the free access to Gladsheim that rank provides."

Finn had been sipping his tea. He choked, his eyes going wide.

"Excuse me?" he spluttered.

I bit the inside of my cheek and swore. We'd reached Morgana despite Snorri's best efforts, but even with the card we hadn't gotten the help we'd hoped for. Not only that, Finn had lost everything on top of it.

"Think of it as temporary administrative leave," Morgana said, glancing at me. Her mismatched eyes sparkled, and there was more warmth to her accent than I'd yet heard.

What are you up to, woman?

Morgana whispered a word, a current of power stirring around her. The cheery garden was masked in shadows, adding a strange dullness to the air.

"This is an extremely grave matter that must be kept in utmost secrecy," she said, her voice muffled by the weird darkness. "You are wise to be so cautious. Not even Keymaster MacCauley or the rest of the Althing will be informed. As far as they will know, you are being punished severely for defying my instructions. In reality, I am reassigning you, Finn. To the members of our Order across the world, you will henceforth hold the rank of *hersir*."

Finn's face went pale. "There haven't been any *hersir* since the first World War."

"I'm not familiar with that title," Hasebe said, saving me the trouble. It was another word my gift had chosen not to translate.

"*Hersir* are singular wizards capable of carrying out special objectives with great discretion and secrecy," Morgana replied, looking solemnly at Finn. "They often end up hand-picking teams of operatives for the purpose of eliminating great threats to our Order. The last one was my predecessor, before she took the position of Morgana."

She turned her mismatched gaze back on me, the aura of her authority almost a physical being. "Hersir Aalto, the Third of this cycle is going to need a teacher if she is to aid in your assignment. Is that a responsibility you'd be willing to accept?"

I glanced at Finn, finding him looking back at me.

"Only if she gets to make the decision about becoming part of the Order or not when all's said and done," Finn said. "I'll train her, but as a private tutor and not as a master of the White Order. You know, since I'm banished and all that."

Something resembling a smirk worked its way across Morgana's face. "Very well."

"And the group doesn't have to be solely wizards," Finn added. "The most successful attack we got on Odin was with a revolver."

Hasebe snickered, holding his teacup in both hands.

"I suppose that makes sense as well," Morgana said. "I fear sometimes we're too fixated on the transmundane."

I tried not to stare at the pair while the conversation progressed. Morgana was proving to be more down-to-earth than expected. Or perhaps it was that bloody card.

What hold does that ace have over her that she's giving him carte blanche? Is it the threat Odin poses to her power, or is it something else?

With their arrangements made, Finn and I began to run Morgana through the events of the past few days. We detailed as much as we knew about what Nic had done in Bergen and the torture he'd sustained at the hands of Odin while crafting Gleipnir. I still found myself hoping it was just Odin and not Cari who'd injured him.

Morgana's expression remained grave and stoic as we talked, but her odd eyes betrayed her again. She was more worried than I'd seen her.

As we finished our accounts, Morgana waved a hand, dispelling the stifling shadows. We'd finished our tea by then, which gave me a much-needed dose of home amidst the escalating strangeness of the week.

The four of us stood as several Keepers filed into the room. Morgana nodded, her expression polite. "I can't offer you any respite, I'm afraid. Appearances must be kept. Miss Gilkeson is not technically a member of our Order."

"I appreciate the thought," I said, "but I've some affairs back in Knightsbridge that must be attended to before anything else."

The affairs in question were a warm bath and a good sleep, though I wouldn't tell her that.

"That's your business, then," Morgana said. "Wizard Aalto, will you be accompanying her?"

"I think I've got to at this point," Finn said. He shot me an odd look. "She needs some questions answered."

"Understood." She leaned in to whisper, "Keep me apprised of your progress through our private channels. You know the ones I mean. This must be handled as swiftly as possible."

Finn tipped his head in a brief nod. "Of course, Morgana. We'll be off, then."

We exchanged contact information, then Finn, Hasebe, and I set off. None of us spoke as the Keepers led us through the confusing maze of torchlit passageways. We were joined halfway by a bandaged Nic, smelling strongly of medicinal herbs.

"That went well," he said, glib as ever. I was grateful to hear more life in his voice. "But I've got to get back to San Diego. Jerica gets nervous when I'm away for too long."

"Talk later," Finn said. "We've got a lot of work to do."

Nic nodded, turning off down a different corridor.

Gladstone was absent from the stairway atrium this time, but in his place was Keeper Jurgen holding a small trunk.

"I'm not sure what you did to weasel out of punishment," said Keeper Jurgen, "but Morgana insisted I send this with you."

"*Uruz,*" Finn murmured, gesturing up with one finger. The trunk floated off the floor and trailed behind us. I didn't blame him. I didn't think any of us felt like carrying the thing.

I called Westaway from the church and had him meet us on Videy Island with the aircar, rather than going all the way back to Reykjavik's airhub. It was probably breaking an air travel law, but I didn't care.

Hasebe elected to ride in the front cab with Westaway, leaving me alone with Finn for the first time since our conversation in San Diego.

"Well?" I asked after we'd taken flight.

"Well what?"

I rolled my eyes. "Don't play dumb, Aalto. What is that card?"

"It's my ace," he said, flipping the skull ace between his fingers.

"I can see that. What's so important about it that the grand master of your order let you run free with favours, no questions asked, as soon as she saw it? We both know the so-called banishment is only for show."

Finn snorted. "No, she does mean that part. Fortunately for us, there are far more magical resources available than just Gladsheim. It's just a convenient central location for much of our Order."

He slid the card back up his sleeve. "Lía gave me my ace at the Lock, right when I first started on with her. Told me it was my one use, get-out-of-anything free card. Even though my magic showed up on its own, because I was Morgana's apprentice, we had to do everything as traditional and by-the-book as possible."

Finn leaned back in the padded seat, kicking his feet up atop the trunk. "Meaning I still got Drowned, but all it did was amplify what was already there."

"And the card?" I pressed.

Finn let out a long breath. "You Drowned, so I suppose you know. There's always some sort of vision during the process. It's different for everyone. Lía told me she saw an elk that turned into a young woman wearing a crown of antlers."

"I know someone who saw a scene straight from a comic book," I said, thinking back. "Not Cari. An old friend. She wasn't much up on mythology, but Thor comic books held a certain charm for her."

"That's the common thread," Finn said. "A connection to mythological or cultural figures of magical power. Every wizard's vision I've ever heard of had that. Except mine."

He shifted forward, resting his hands on his knees. "I saw myself in a forest, chasing after someone in a white hooded cloak. A girl, I thought, from the figure. Never could catch up to her, no matter how hard or fast I ran.

"She got to the top of a hill I couldn't climb up. That's when she turned to look at me and pulled her hood back. I saw her face."

Finn looked me square in the eyes. "She had long black hair tied in a braid, and the most piercing grey eyes I've ever seen. I thought she was a princess or something from the way she carried herself. Noble jawline, high rosy cheeks, the works. Weirdest part was, she had tattoos all up one arm."

The bottom fell out of my stomach. "That's..."

"I had no idea who she was. Neither did Lía, but she thought the girl must be important if she was in my Drowning vision. So she gave me the skull ace and told me if I ever found the girl in my vision, I could show her the card and she'd hear me out."

Blood drained from my face as my mind spun. *That's impossible... I'd had my magic for all of a year by then...*

"Seven years I've had that ace," Finn said, rubbing the back of his neck. "I'd never seen the girl again in all that time. Until she walked into The Old Bell Tavern four days ago with Snorri and her bodyguard."

No wonder he'd essentially committed treason against his organisation to help me this whole week. That also explained the focus ring I now wore on my index finger. He'd commissioned it from Nic, or at least paid for it. That was what neither of them would tell me in his shop back in San Diego.

"Now... look, I'm not telling you any of this because I want something from you," Finn said. "I never believed in the whole 'soulmates' thing, before you think it's anything romantic. I still don't know why you're supposed to be important in my life. Maybe it's this whole Odin-Juno business we've gotten mixed up in. I'm not trying to be weird about it, I just... I thought you deserve one person giving it to you straight."

I slumped back in my seat. A week prior, I'd been searching the world for my best friend, desperately hoping I could talk some sense into her.

Now, not only was my best friend missing again, I'd set out to kill the most powerful wizard in the world with the aid of another wizard I barely knew. And somehow I was important to that wizard I barely knew, though he couldn't explain how or why.

I couldn't help it. I started to laugh. Before long I was laughing so hard tears streamed from my eyes and my core muscles ached.

"How is that funny?" Finn said.

"It's not," I said, trying to compose myself. "But this is the second time in my life I've found myself in the middle of a situation that's so absurd I'm not sure it's even real."

I managed to choke back my laughter, wiping my eyes. "I appreciate you telling me. It may not be relevant to our objective, that remains to be seen. Either way, it's good to know. Thank you."

Finn nodded. There was some colour to his cheeks which I chose to overlook.

"I'll have a lot of work to do once we get back to Knightsbridge," I said instead. "I've got an arm to mend and some research into Norse folklore to begin, let alone arranging things with my clients."

"Busy schedule, Ace. Think we can fit killing the Norse god of magic in there somewhere?"

"I think we might just make that happen," I said, reaching for my phone.

CHAPTER TWENTY-THREE

BURNING FENCES, MENDING BRIDGES

KNIGHTSBRIDGE, LONDON

C urrents of wind teased my hair as I leaned against my flat's balcony railing. We'd been home for less than three hours, but after the week's madness, the noise and clamour of London made for a relaxing dose of normal.

I sipped at the glass of wine clutched in my bad hand. The mesh cast would hold until I got to work restoring the broken bone with my magic. But I was drained dry. I'd need a good long sleep before I even thought of using magic again.

"This is a really nice apartment."

I whirled, nearly dropping my glass over the balcony. She'd abandoned the teal vest and the hood, standing there in her charred and bloodied fatigues like some futuristic soldier.

"Really? Two years I've been looking for you, and now you just show up here?"

"It's not like I knew where you lived after I left New York," Cari said. "I've been keeping tabs on that aircar of yours. Still not too many of those around this part of Europe. I just followed it to London and watched to see what landing pad it would go for."

I made a mental note to bring that to Hasebe's attention. If it could even remotely be a security risk, he'd want to know.

"Be that as it may," I said, "why are you here in the first place?"

Cari leaned against the wall, crossing her arms over her chest. "I'd give you some line about reconnecting after all this time or wanting to make sure you're okay, but I don't think you'd believe me."

"That doesn't answer my question," I said. I hadn't seen her in two years, but I still knew my best friend's tells. She was bothered about something but didn't know how to bring it up.

Is she actually going to apologise, or is that too much to hope?

"Alright, fine," Cari sighed. "For as much as he didn't show me, Odin did give me some bits and pieces of magical training. When it was convenient for him, of course."

"Of course," I echoed. "How does it feel to be the apprentice of a mythological figure?"

"Former apprentice," Cari snorted, wincing. "Damn it, don't make me laugh! My nose still hurts. It's only been reset for a couple hours. And to answer your question, it's fantastic. I love almost being murdered by someone I read stories about for half my life. If you and Bluey and Hasebe hadn't been there..."

She trailed off, looking away. "I guess that means I should thank you or something."

"Only if you want to."

"Don't make this harder than it is, Brooke. The point is, Odin is crazy powerful. Between him and his brothers, the three of them practically created magic like we know it today."

My fingers tightened on the wine glass. "Does that mean we'll have to kill three godlike men instead of just one?"

"No. Near as I can tell, Odin is the only one still alive. He said he'd heard rumours of Thor kicking around Thailand somewhere, but never bothered to follow through. Most of the ancient Aesir wizards are dead and gone decades over."

Cari clenched her jaw. "No, this is bad enough with only one magical demigod trying to kill me."

"I thought he was fully a—"

"It doesn't matter, alright?" Cari's hair flared into strands of blue fire. "All of it was a lie anyway. Odin was never a hero, the Aesir and Vanir weren't gods, and the stories I idolised for so long mean nothing. All that matters is what we're doing here and now."

"Which is killing Odin," I said, trying to read between the lines.

"Which is making sure I don't die. If Odin could scry or perform divination at all, I'd probably be gone already. That's the one thing the Order is good for, preventing everyone but themselves from doing forbidden magic."

I decided to let that sleeping dog alone. "Do you still have Gleipnir?"

Cari nodded. "Gonna be keeping that close from now on. If all else fails, Gleipnir might buy me just enough time to choose how I want to die."

"Still a fatalist, I see. That hasn't changed."

It struck me then, the thing Cari wasn't telling me.

She was *scared*.

Odin's casual betrayal and near-murder of my best friend had cut her far more deeply than she was admitting.

"Cari, what do you want from me?" I asked, more bluntly than I meant. I was still exhausted. "You've been dancing around it for five minutes now."

She was silent for a long moment. Then Cari relaxed against the wall, her hair shifting to its normal coffee brown again.

Such an odd sight... I'd nearly forgotten how weird that looked.

"We are going to do it, right?" Cari asked, her voice small. "We are going to kill Odin?"

Despite myself, my heart twinged. This wasn't Juno, terror of the Keepers and mysterious rogue *seidhkona* asking the question. This was Carissa Edwards, the lonely little girl I'd exchanged letters with until both of us got email addresses. The realisation drove my stubborn hope for my best friend, despite everything.

I turned to face her fully. Cari's eyes were defiant, proud, but I could still see the fear in them.

"You're damn right we are," I said. I threw back the last of my wine in a single swallow, pulling my phone from my back pocket. It was battered and scratched, but powered on when I pressed the button. "But not without a couple of old friends."

Her eyes widened. "You can't seriously want to bring Amy in on this."

"Not your old friends, dummy. Mine."

TO BE CONTINUED

HOW TO SAY THESE WORDS

*O*ld Norse is an incredibly cool language, but it's not a Latinate language (meaning it's not descended from the same language family as Latin) and can be tricky for people unfamiliar with it – hence, a pronunciation guide and a fun fact for each. Just for fun, try to roll the 'r's in these words – that's how they would have been pronounced twelve hundred years ago (we think, there's a lot of room for interpretation)

RUNE NAMES

Ansuz (AHN-sooz) - Rune name, can mean "Odin." 4th rune in the Elder Futhorc (the Old Norse alphabet), modern letter 'A'

Berkana (BEHR-kah-nah) - Rune name, can mean "birch tree." 18th rune in the Elder Futhorc, modern letter 'B'

Ehwaz (AYE-wahz) - Rune name, can mean "horse." 19th rune in the Elder Futhorc, modern letter 'E'

Fehu (FEY-who) - Rune name, can mean "wealth." 1st rune in the Elder Futhorc, modern letter 'F'

Isa (EYE-suh) - Rune name, can mean "ice." 11th rune in the Elder Futhorc, modern letter 'I'

Jera (YEE-ruh) - Rune name, can mean "year." 12th rune in the Elder Futhorc, modern letter 'J'

Kenaz (KEY-nahz) - Rune name, can mean "torch." 6th rune in the Elder Futhorc, modern letter 'K'

Laguz (LAH-gooz) - Rune name, can mean "water." 21st rune in the Elder Futhorc, modern letter 'L'

Mannaz (MAH-nahz) - Rune name, can mean "humanity." 20th rune in the Elder Futhorc, modern letter 'M'

Othala (OH-thah-lah) - Rune name, can mean "inheritance." 24th rune in the Elder Futhorc, modern letter 'O'

Raidho (RYE-doh) - Rune name, can mean "wagon." 5th rune in the Elder Futhorc, modern letter 'R'

Sowilo (SO-wee-low) - Rune name, can mean "sun." 16th rune in the Elder Futhorc, modern letter 'S'

Uruz (OO-rooz) - Rune name, can mean "bull." 2nd rune in the Elder Futhorc, modern letter 'U'

OTHER WORDS

Argr (AHR-grr) - Old Norse word meaning "coward." One of the worst insults you could give a man of that era

Fylgja (FILL juh) - Old Norse word for a guardian spirit. Sometimes appears as an animal, sometimes thought to be a part of the soul

Hersir (HER-seer) - Old Norse title referring to the commander of a small army. A title of military rank as well as nobility, hersir usually answered to a jarl or lord of some kind

Merr (MARE) - Old Norse word meaning "mare," as in a female horse. Also a serious insult

Seidhkona (SAYTH-koh-nuh) - Old Norse word literally meaning "sorcery-wife." More akin to the modern English word "witch" or "sorceress"

<u>Videyjarkyrkja (VEE-day-yarr-Keer-kyuh)</u> – Old Norse name meaning "Church of Videy," which itself translates to "island of trees." Videy is an island just off the coast of Reykjavik

THANKS!

It's been a long journey to get here – you guys reading this won't know the half of it. But honestly, thanks for reading this book! I hope there will be many more to come after this one. I couldn't do this without you.

My eyes were opened to the world of storytelling when I was five, making up stuff for a competition (and doing it all by myself, unlike some of my peers!). As I got older, I saw more and more how good stories connect with us – they show us worlds where regular people overcome their problems, succeed despite all odds, and give us hope that maybe we too can face our boring problems in the real world.

I'd like to give some thanks to some of the people who believed in me over the years:

Jeff, for being open-minded enough to let me explore the English language and sparking a deep love of words; Ally, for cutting through my Gordian knots with simple logic and helping me shape this world into something beautiful; Chad, for being my first true writing buddy (and teaching me how to use Photoshop, you're a lifesaver!); Kary, for challenging me to think like an entrepreneur instead of just a creative; and Abi, for believing in me when no one else did (even me).

We've all been given gifts, and I'm seeking to use mine for the glory of my Creator by writing the best books I can.

Hope you enjoyed *The Dove and the Raven*, and I'll see you in the next project!

May the pages rise up to meet you,

Ian Henderson

www.ingramcontent.com/pod-product-compliance
Lightning Source LLC
Chambersburg PA
CBHW060317260626
47160CB00007B/2641